WAR CHANT

WAR CHANT

By DEE DUNSING

Decorations by E. Harper Johnson

JD 9223 w

LONGMANS, GREEN AND CO.

NEW YORK · LONDON · TORONTO

1954

LONGMANS, GREEN AND CO., INC.
55 FIFTH AVENUE, NEW YORK 3

LONGMANS, GREEN AND CO. LTD.
6 & 7 CLIFFORD STREET, LONDON W 1

LONGMANS, GREEN AND CO.
215 VICTORIA STREET, TORONTO 1

WAR CHANT

PUBLISHED SIMULTANEOUSLY IN THE DOMINION OF CANADA BY
LONGMANS, GREEN AND CO., TORONTO

FIRST EDITION

LIBRARY OF CONGRESS CATALOG CARD NUMBER 54-7679

Printed in the United States of America

Thank You!

My thanks are due:

The University of Oklahoma Press and Grant Foreman for permission to quote from Grant Foreman's *Indian Removal;* Miss Audrey Broward of the Jacksonville (Florida) Public Library for help with research; Dr. Dorothy Dodd of Tallahassee for suggestions concerning Floridiana in an earlier book, *Swamp Shadows;* William Byron Mowery of Warwick, New York, author, for use of his Novel Pre-Comp, O. S. Wodrich of Jacksonville, and Constance Hendricks and Gwen Youngblood of Long Beach, California, for general criticisms of *War Chant* in first draft.

DEE DUNSING
Jacksonville, Fla.

Contents

WAR CHANT

Chapter 1

Shakochee

"In the dishonorable record of our dealings with
the Indians, there is perhaps no blacker chapter
than that relating to the Seminole people."

—GRANT FOREMAN
in *Indian Removal*

It was dark in the Florida woods, except where the midafternoon sun struck through in dazzling patterns that lighted the forest trail. Rod Wheeler walked softly in his worn moccasins, leaving hardly any track in the damp carpet of rotting oak leaves. His eyes, sharply blue, watched the birds in the tops of the towering trees. His ears listened to their talk, which he knew almost as well as the talk of people.

He was dressed like a frontiersman, in long deerskin shirt, tightly belted, and rakish coonskin cap. Slung carelessly in the crook of his arm was his Kentucky rifle. Although the gun was old and its flintlock mechanism not the best in the Territory, he cherished it.

Usually he carried a bag of rabbits or quail, or something he was bringing home for the family table, but today his haul was better—silver coins. The soldiers at Fort Brooke on Tampa Bay and the friendly Indians camping near by had bought his entire stock of carved lucky pieces. And now the Indians were calling him "Luckmaker" because one such talisman had deflected a bullet and saved the life of a brave.

1

It made Rod smile to think of being "Luckmaker," for he himself did not much believe in the power of charms and it was purely for fun that he liked to wear a wooden eagle on a thong around his neck. But he was proud of the silver coins. In the past he had been able to swap his trinkets only for things of dubious value, such as broken knives or fossil shark's teeth.

Getting real money for his work made him seem less a boy and more a man. And deep in Rod's heart was the wish to be full-grown so he could take his place beside his father.

He caught the honeyed trill of a pine warbler and puckered up his mouth to answer, but paused, pierced by a sudden fear. Maybe the call was an Indian signal. This morning his father had said, "Keep a sharp eye out for Indians, son. Those at the post will be friendly, but the others are putting on their war paint. Watch for them."

Rod himself knew of the brewing storm in this autumn of 1835, for Seminoles and Mikasukies had been ordered to leave Florida and make new homes west of the Mississippi. It was said that five chiefs—Holasti, Emathla, Fucaluste, Hajo and Charley E-Mathlar—were willing to sail at the appointed time, but the others, led by Osceola, had vowed they would die in their native land. And they had launched an ultimatum to the peaceful chiefs: Stay with us or we will kill you.

Matters had grown even worse during the summer, when the fiery Osceola was put in irons by the Indian agent for "back talk," and when in August a messenger riding between Forts King and Brooke was deliberately murdered, it was like the first muttering thunder from a swiftly clouding sky. There were other war-weather signs—cabins burned, hunting parties fired upon, and a sudden increase in the purchase of ammunition by the Indians.

All these thoughts cast a shadow over Rod's mood as he listened for the bird trill to come again. At last it sounded—high-pitched, a flutelike purr. Surely it was the call of a real pine warbler. But the boy was cautious and did not answer.

The oak hammock thinned to a growth of pine, magnolias and cabbage palms, their trunks wrapped with vines, their branches dripping gray Spanish moss. Everywhere were signs of a shy, half-secret woods' life—the flutter of feathered wings in the treetops, the rattle of dead palmetto, where a lizard or a mouse moved faster than the eye, and the quick flirt of a squirrel's tail against the lichen-grayed bark of a live oak.

To the right of the trail a sturdy grapevine swarmed over the scrub, its broad leaves reaching into a pine.

Some deep-buried impulse urged Rod to go more slowly. He could not say what alarmed him. The forest seemed as placid as ever. But as he neared the vine he halted, startled by a sound that rose out of its depths.

What it was, he couldn't make out. Heart pounding, he waited. Again he heard it—smaller than the brushing of wind in the treetops, but clear and distinct. It was not the rattle of a snake, nor the growl of a wildcat, nor the cry of any animal Rod knew.

Again it came. This time his skin prickled with fear as he recognized that the noise was human—harsh breathing, or perhaps a groan.

Automatically he drew back the hammer of his rifle, raised the gun muzzle so that it covered the vines.

"Come out of there!"

His words rang loudly in the empty woods and rolled back to him as an echo. There was no sound from the grapevine.

He waited, uncertain. In spite of his rifle, he felt little security. The advantage belonged to that fellow under the vine. He would get the first shot. But as seconds rolled by, Rod began to think maybe the stranger was afraid, too.

The idea gave him courage. Resolutely he took several steps forward and parted the leaves with his gun muzzle.

To his surprise, he saw a boy's scared, hostile face. Even in the leaf shadows, Rod could see the gag of rawhide parting the lips and a big, discolored lump that bulged from the red-brown skin of the boy's forehead. His arms were tied, and his ankles.

"Shakochee!" breathed Rod, shaky with relief but shocked to find his friend here. "What's happened?" Rod laid down his gun and drew his hunting knife. In a second he had cut all the thongs.

Shakochee sat up instantly, wet his stiff lips and replied, "Slave catcher."

Rod stared, puzzled. "Sam Ruther?"

Shakochee nodded with vigor. "And Dan'l. They ask me guide them to Withlacoochee Cove. But they not want to go there," he added bitterly.

"Why did they tie you?"

In Shakochee's eyes there was a mixture of pride and hurt as he returned Rod's gaze. But he did not flinch at the explanation.

"I have a strong back. They would take me to Savannah as slave."

Rod was too surprised to speak. He could hardly believe that Ruther—callous and mean-natured as he was—would dare enslave a full-blooded Seminole. But as he gazed at his friend, he realized that Shakochee was as dark as many Negroes. Ruther could lie about his race, and the boy's protests would be ignored, for already the slave catchers had imprisoned and sold many Indians with Negro blood. They had been bold enough even to take Osceola's wife, in spite of the warrior's grief and threats.

Rod spoke in soft anger. "My father hates Sam Ruther. Last year he fought him—with his bare fists. He told me to keep out of his way or I might get shot."

"I will take his life," said Shakochee somberly.

"No," protested Rod. "No, Shakochee. That would get you

in trouble—and all the Seminoles. Let him alone. He'll get paid back sometime."

Shakochee did not answer or seem to hear, and Rod looked toward the trail ahead. "Let's get out," he urged, "before they come to get you."

The Indian boy started to rise, but paused, on his knees, one hand against the earth. His face took on a faraway look, as he listened intently.

Rod listened, too. At first he heard nothing. Then his ear picked up a faint, rhythmic thump.

"Ruther!"

He grabbed his gun and jumped to his feet. Shakochee, quicker than he, was already bounding across the trail. Together they ran swiftly through the fern carpet beneath the big old oaks. Where a bough hung low, Rod swung up onto it and clambered to the tree's top. There he straddled a branch, putting a ragged curtain of Spanish moss between himself and the trail.

Shakochee had paused to straighten up a telltale broken fern; now he, too, scaled a tree near Rod's, and the two of them waited silently.

Soon the hoofbeats thudded loud, and through the leaves Rod glimpsed a red roan on the trail. The horse slowed and stopped beside the grapevine. Rod recognized its stocky little rider by the jut of his nose beneath the coonskin cap and the fine featherwork on his leather jacket and moccasins.

The slaver did not dismount, but looked impatiently back along the trail. At last a big Negro rode up on a long-tailed Indian pony, slid off and approached the roan.

"You mighty smart, suh," the black man chuckled. "You pick jest zackly where we leavum."

Ruther ignored the flattery. "Drag him out and haul him up to the stockade," he said sharply. "See that he's tied good and tight till I get there—he's slippery as goose grease."

Rod's pulse hammered in his throat, but the corners of his mouth turned upward in a faint smile. "Slippery as goose grease!" What would they say when they looked under the vine!

Dan'l moved toward the grape canopy, the sun gleaming on his bare, sweaty shoulders and spraying light from a quiver of white-tipped arrows slung across his back. Rod noted those arrows absently, realizing in the back of his mind that they were unusual—for everyone carried a rifle, except those Indians whose weapons had been taken away because they hunted outside their reservation.

The black man swept back the leaves and bent forward to grasp his young captive. There was an instant of surprised silence. Then he said, "He gone, suh!"

Ruther stiffened. "Gone! He can't be!"

"He do be gone," asserted Dan'l.

The slaver's eyes flicked across the woods. "This is the right place," he said at last, his voice as hard as granite. "I made note of that down pine over there."

For answer Dan'l held out a bit of the leather thong that had bound Shakochee.

Ruther reached for the rawhide and examined it. "Cut clean through," he noted coldly. "Anything else?"

Both men scanned the ground in the area of the vine, and suddenly Ruther pointed his gold-ringed hand. "What's that—over there in the tall grass?"

Dan'l turned, took a few steps through the scrub, and picked up a small object that flashed red in his fingers.

Misgivings smote Rod. Had Shakochee dropped something?

"Eagle," said Dan'l, handing the object to his master. "Lucky eagle."

Rod's hand trembled as he reached for his own lucky piece

and grasped only the dangling thong. He glanced toward the Indian in the neighboring oak and saw Shakochee eying him gravely.

Ruther was turning the eagle over and over. "Ever see it before?"

"It belongs Luckmaker," replied Dan'l, proud of his knowledge. "I see him round Luckmaker's neck."

Rod clung hard to the tree limb and wished he had never thought of whittling the charm—any charm. For if he had carved his initials in a tree trunk, he could not have said more plainly who had released Shakochee. He hoped that Dan'l did not know his name and would have to ask about him at the fort.

"And who's Luckmaker?" inquired Ruther sourly.

"Boy name Rod Wheeler," spouted Dan'l. "Live up Hillsborough River."

Rod bit his lip hard. He thought of what his father had said about Sam Ruther: "He'd as soon kill a man in the deep woods, where no one could see, as shoot a wild turkey for supper."

Ruther handed the charm back to Dan'l. "Keep it for luck. *He* ain't going to have no luck himself, from now on. Cutting loose slaves won't do—not in the Territory!"

He wheeled his horse and started back along the trail, but drew up short and called to Dan'l. "Take a look around before you follow. They might be close by."

"Yessuh."

Ruther gouged the roan into a gallop, while Dan'l obediently began to paw the grapevine in a search for Rod or Shakochee. He did it gingerly, however, as if he remembered that the white boy carried a gun.

Soon after his master's horse was out of sight, Dan'l came back to the path. It was plain he didn't want to press the hunt. But, as if seized by a sudden thought, he stared up into the oaks, shading his eyes with his hand. For a fear-laden moment, Rod watched him scan the treetops. At last he shrugged, climbed onto the back of his pony and started slowly along the trail.

Rod waited, his heart knocking hard against the rough bark of the oak. When the sound of the pony's hoofs had died away, he swung downward from branch to branch until he stood on the ground. Shakochee was there before him.

"I'm sorry I dropped the charm," said Rod sheepishly. "But we're lucky he didn't find us."

Shakochee nodded.

"Come home with me," Rod urged. "My mother can doctor that bump on your forehead."

Again Shakochee nodded "Yes."

As they returned to the trail and loped along it toward the Wheeler farm, the Indian boy did not speak. Rod knew he was grateful but that he would show his thanks by a deed rather than with talk.

He did offer one remark, after a long time. "Your charm is good," he said. "It kept Dan'l from seeing us. Only now he will wear it himself, and we will have bad luck."

"It'll never work for Dan'l," said Rod indignantly.

"No? Can it then work still for you?"

"Yes, it will work for me," assured Rod, adding honestly, "if it works for anybody."

"It must be fine to own such a charm," remarked Shakochee.

Rod glanced at him quickly. He was always surprised at the great faith the Indians had in his baubles. To them they were as powerful as guns.

"I have a good carving of a bear at home," he said. "I'll give it to you, Shakochee."

The Indian did not reply, but Rod noticed the smile of pleasure that touched his mouth.

Mrs. Wheeler daubed gently with a vinegar-soaked rag at

the bump on Shakochee's forehead while Rod told what had happened.

"Ruther!" she exclaimed, her bright-blue eyes hard with repressed anger. "It's men like him that cause most of our troubles in the Territory."

She went to her dish cupboard and opened it, revealing a great array of dried roots and herbs, as well as bottles filled with dark medicines. Rod waited for her to choose the right one, confident she could treat any illness as well as a doctor, for he had seen her "cure up" many a settler along the Hillsborough River.

She took down the bottle of bitters—a homemade distillation of dewberry, wild cherry, sumac root and brandy—and poured a spoonful. Matter-of-factly she pinched Shakochee's nostrils together while she thrust the spoon into his mouth. Rod tried not to smile at the involuntary drawing of the Indian's lips, for he himself had taken the bitters often and knew how bad they tasted.

"I'm not pleased, either, Rod, that you should get onto the wrong side of Sam Ruther," she said dourly. "There's bad blood between him and your father already."

"Yes, Ma, I know." Rod agreed, his face serious. "But it was nothing I did on purpose. I had to help Shakochee."

"Yes, son," his mother answered kindly. She turned her attention to Rod's two younger brothers, Hughie, thirteen, and Dovvy, eight, as they came tramping into the house.

"You're all through in the field, boys?" she asked quickly. It was plain she had not expected to see them so early.

"Yes, Ma," replied Dovvy, looking curiously at Shakochee, but not asking questions.

"Is your father coming too?"

Hughie stared at the Indian, but answered his mother's question. "Hart Whitley rode up and Pa said we could quit early. They're comin' in, too."

"You'd best go, Shakochee," said the woman swiftly, corking up the bottle of bitters and returning it to the shelf. "Mr. Wheeler wouldn't like us getting tangled with Mr. Ruther in any way—of that I'm sure. And especially if somebody's with him today to hear what happened. Rod, hand the boy that bit of bread and meat you've put up for him and take him through the grove to the woods."

Rod reached quickly for the food and beckoned Shakochee toward the front door. Together they walked hastily through the orange grove to the woods. Inside its dark shelter, Rod paused, stuck his hand in his pocket and fished out the charm he had promised his friend.

"Here," was all he said, not wanting it to seem as if he were giving a great thing.

Shakochee reached out his hand and took the small carving of the bear. He handled it reverently, looking at it with great interest, and letting it roll over in his palm so that he could see the carving on all sides and the red and black paint used to color it.

His eyes glowed when he raised them, and his smile was gentle. "Good for halist-chaway!" he said in his guttural English.

"The Indians at the fort buy them," explained Rod, pleased that Shakochee had said his gift was good for a medicine bag.

"For halist-chaway!" repeated Shakochee. He wheeled suddenly, leaped over a bit of fallen timber and ran off into the woods. For a second Rod watched him weave through the trees, then he was gone. The woods where he had been were silent and still, except for the rustle of wind in the pine tops and the occasional swaying of a bit of moss.

Later the whole family sat grouped around Hart Whitley in front of the big hearth, while the cook fire died away to a glow, and the chill of evening crept into the room. Mrs. Wheeler sat to one side, mending a homespun shirt. Rod, Hughie and

Dovvy were cross-legged on the floor, separating cotton from its seeds, but listening to what the grown folks were saying. Next to the "company," on one of the dining benches, Mr. Wheeler pondered the visitor's words, his chin in his work-grimed hand, his strong face grave.

Hart Whitley had brought news so startling that Rod forgot his adventure of the afternoon and Shakochee's brief visit. Charley E-Mathlar, a friendly chief, had been murdered. He was the first to bring in his cattle, selling them and taking gold in return, so that his band would be ready to sail for the west. His body was found, stabbed many times. The gold pieces lay scattered around him.

"It's more than murder," observed Mr. Wheeler softly. "It's the Indians' first real attack against us whites. It means they're not going to be shipped west—they're going to fight."

"They've planned it for a long time," Hart agreed somberly. "But this is a bold move, typical of Osceola." He stretched his long legs toward the fire, so that the warmth struck against the soles of his moccasins. "Osceola meant to scare the friendly chiefs, and that's just what he's done. Some of them have been sitting on the fence, wondering what way to jump. They're on his side now."

Rod looked up at the scout, whose skin was burned almost as dark as the leather of his hunter's jacket. The boy had known Hart since he came to Fort Brooke eight months ago, but others remembered how he had come into the Territory nine years before with a blanket roll on his back to homestead near Tallahassee. Although he owned a small plantation, some premonition had made him come south to offer his woods knowledge to the Army. For he had long been saying there would be an Indian war, although people were just beginning to listen.

"What will happen next?" asked Rod.

"What I've always said—a war," Hart replied.

Mr. Wheeler made no comment, but Mrs. Wheeler yanked

angrily at her mending, and Rod knew she was thinking un-
kind thoughts about both Seminoles and certain whites.

"Maybe the friendly Indians will hide and wait for the
trouble to blow over," suggested Rod.

Hart shook his head. "Sometimes I try to imagine that I'm
an Indian—my old friend Lo-Chaw, maybe," he said slowly.
"Lo-Chaw used to be strong for peace. I try to think how he
feels today, down there among his people. Is he still for treaties
with white men? I doubt it. He hated what was done at Payne's
Landing—said we broke our earlier promises. I think he's gathering his warriors to fight."

"Will they paint their faces?" inquired Dovvy.

Hart nodded. "They'll paint themselves red and black and
put on their war plumes. Then they'll dance, chanting, and
beating their war drums. Then—attack."

Mr. Wheeler shook his head, as if to rid it of bad thoughts.
"They do not fight like white men."

"How else could they fight?" countered Hart swiftly.
"They're a few thousand against the force of the whole United
States. Their only chance is to strike from ambush and retreat
when luck's against them. It'll be like fighting ghosts. Maybe
we'll never really defeat them."

"Never?" asked Hughie breathlessly, his gray eyes as round
as the porringers in the cabinet.

Hart hesitated. "Yes—I'll say never."

Mr. Wheeler folded his arms thoughtfully. "We're all in
danger here—so far from the fort. We could build a stockade—
but we'd have few to defend it."

"Not enough," said Mrs. Wheeler quickly. "We'd better stay
in Tampa with Uncle Ace."

Her husband nodded. "You, Hughie, and Dovvy had best go
soon and I'll come later. If I'm needed at the fort . . ."

"There are plenty of soldiers there," Mrs. Wheeler interrupted.

"Not plenty, Mrs. Wheeler," interposed Hart. "And General Clinch at Fort King still has a very small army—not half big enough to defend the Territory. Unless the Secretary of War sends troops right away, the settlers will be fighting by themselves."

"I see," said Mrs. Wheeler, her lips tight. "When do you want us to go in, Will?"

"Tomorrow."

A great wish to help was surging inside Rod, but he did not know what he could do. If he were older, like Hart, he could be a scout. He could find his way through the woods now, and get along anywhere, with a gun and hunting knife. But he did not know the trails to the east. Besides, he was afraid his father would say "No," to any such suggestion.

After a time Mr. Wheeler spoke reflectively, gazing into the fire: "It appears to me we white men have done wrong in putting aside the Treaty of Fort Moultrie. The Indians' time in the Territory is not yet up, and still we order them to go west. Just because we have made a new treaty with some of the chiefs is no honest excuse for moving the entire nation. I cannot find a good reason for this war that is coming."

Rod spoke up: "They say at the fort, Pa, the Indians haven't kept the Treaty of Fort Moultrie."

Hart shot him a glance and said something Rod was always to remember: "Each side will have an argument. And if you listen long enough, each can prove he's right. It's always that way."

The fire was burning low. It was time the Wheelers went to bed. Mrs. Wheeler motioned the boys toward the ladder that led to the loft, where their mattresses lay.

"One thing more," said Mr. Wheeler, holding up a hand. "I have a word to say to Rod—you, too, Mother."

Rod waited, tense. He could feel that something important was in the air. But he was not prepared for what came.

"Hart has asked that Rod come with him to the fort. He can learn things that will make him of use in the time ahead. It will be one of us Wheelers in the Army."

"Will—" Mrs. Wheeler's protest began, but died on her lips. "Yes, of course," she finished, "Rod could be of help."

Rod said nothing. He could not speak. He was too excited and proud. "One of us Wheelers." The words pealed through him like notes of the bugle at Fort Brooke. People couldn't call him "the oldest Wheeler boy" any more. He was no longer someone to be protected. He was nearly grown. Soon he could have his wish—could stand shoulder to shoulder beside his father. For he had been called on to fight.

Chapter II

The Message

"You have guns, and so have we. You have powder and lead, and so have we. You have men and so have we. Your men will fight, and so will ours, till the last drop of the Seminole's blood has moistened the dust of his hunting ground."

—Letter from Osceola to General Clinch in January, 1836

Rod took a persimmon from the small hoard in his pocket and sank his teeth into its frost-sweetened flesh. All during his ride along the trail he had been uneasy, had held his gun across the front of his saddle, ready for a quick shot. He kept thinking about Sam Ruther and Dan'l, and the sunny woods did not seem friendly as they once had been.

He stroked the lucky piece on a thong around his neck—an eagle exactly like the one he had lost—and wondered what Major Belton, commanding officer at Fort Brooke, would want him to do. Hart carried messages, he knew, or scouted out sections of the country for signs of Indian activity. Perhaps they would teach their new recruit to do the same.

Although war had not been declared, the murder of Charley E-Mathlar was accepted by everyone in the Territory as a sure sign that the Indians would fight. Some might come to Fort Brooke in December to board schooners in the bay. But Os-

ceola's men would not, that was certain. Just how many others
they could influence was unknown.

An oak hammock lay ahead. Rod gripped his gun tighter,
as he gazed at the junglelike growth of live oak, sweet bay and
glossy-leaved magnolias that crowded near the water, their
limbs smothered with vines, their branches dripping gray moss.
Here lay the danger of ambush. But he entered the close-grown
oak woods and emerged again without adventure.

The trail edged close to the river. Dazzles of sunshine flashed
along the surface of the water, and from the bay ahead came
a faint smell of salt. A Florida jay flirted its brilliant blue
across the path, and on a tree branch a cardinal whistled.

Rod whistled back, his call close and true. The cardinal replied, Rod answered, and the two kept up a conversation until
Rod had passed the spot.

Through the trees appeared the pine-log stockade of Fort
Brooke, its bright flag floating in the Gulf breeze. Set between
the Hillsborough River and Tampa Bay, the fort was the nu-
cleus of a settlement called Tampa, as yet only a few scattered
cabins. A number of small fishing boats were anchored in the
river, and out in the bay lay a schooner that had brought salt
and would take back cotton.

As Rod came closer he could see blue-clad soldiers sitting in
the shade of the stockade, whittling and talking, while others
fished in the river. Several had dropped lines from a flat-bot-
tomed boat offshore.

Rod's eyes searched for Hart Whitley, but could not find
him. He was sorry, for Hart was more than just a soldier whom
he admired—he was a friend. The two had much in common—
their love of the lakes and swamps and jagged coast line of
Florida, their ability to sustain themselves in the woods like
Indians, and their skill in imitating birds and woods animals.

Outside the stockade gate, Rod shouted "hello" to the guard
and inquired after Hart.

"Think he's down at his tent," replied the guard, who knew Rod.

The boy rode along the edge of the stockade to where a cluster of tents faced the river, and approached the one shared by Hart and a soldier named John Fox.

Only Fox was there, sitting cross-legged on a bit of canvas while he cleaned his gun with lazy deliberation. He was medium tall and slender, with sharp, straight shoulders that matched the knifelike jab of his blue eyes.

Rod had met him before and been impressed by his talk of politics, the Army and philosophy. Fox had said the administration at Washington neglected Florida in order to electioneer and that the United States was "cheating the fool savages" with the Treaty of Payne's Landing.

But today he was in no talking mood. He looked up at Rod, said "hello" and returned to his gun cleaning.

"I was looking for Hart Whitley," ventured Rod.

"Not here," replied Fox shortly.

"I'm going to stay—work with the Army," burst out Rod, unable to keep the news.

"So I heard."

The terse answer and the silence that followed struck Rod like a dash of cold water. He opened his mouth to speak, but closed it, realizing that this fellow didn't care if he came into the Army or stayed home.

Hurt and angry, Rod turned away, only to hear his name called. When he looked in the direction of the voice, he saw Hart Whitley striding toward him.

This greeting was different. The scout's gray eyes were friendly and his handshake warm. "Ready to join us, Rod?"

"All ready, sir."

"I'm glad you've come. Let's see the major."

This was more like it. As they swung into step, Rod regained his sense of importance and excitement. Even if the others didn't pay much attention, Hart valued his abilities and would teach him to be a real scout. Some day the Army would consider him a good man in its service—not just a frontier boy.

When they faced Major Belton in the main building of the fort, Rod was as taut as a racehorse.

"This is the lad I told you about—Rod Wheeler," Hart introduced him.

The major smiled. "We need a Luckmaker."

The remark took Rod by surprise. "I don't really make luck," he replied, abashed.

"No, but it's an advantage to have the Indians think so."

"Yes, sir." It was an angle that hadn't occurred to Rod.

"Show him his quarters, Hart, and give him orders. I'll leave his training up to you."

"Yes, sir," agreed Hart.

The two saluted and went outside. "You're to be in our tent," Hart said. "There's work around here to do, but mainly I want you to learn a little more about trails from me—mostly those leading toward Fort King. You may be asked to carry messages there. Of course there's the military road that's a direct route, but we scouts can't always travel out in the open."

"Yes, sir."

"First of all, I want to see how you shoot."

Rod was anxious for some definite way to prove his skill. As the two paused beneath the trees, Hart nodded his head toward the top of a tall pine. "See that cone near the tip? Right where that mocker was sitting a minute ago?"

"I see it."

"Try to hit that."

Rod took aim and his bullet exploded the cone.

"Good enough," observed Hart shortly, starting back toward camp.

"Wait," urged Rod.

As the scout paused, Rod reloaded and searched the sky for a flying target. He let a mocking bird pass and ignored a brash pine warbler that sang in a treetop. But when a hawk swooped down out of the sky he trained his sight on it.

"Too far," warned Hart. "You'll only waste your lead."

But Rod stubbornly followed the bird, and when he thought he could hit, squeezed the trigger.

The hawk seemed to pause in mid-air, then sailed majestically out of range.

Rod's hand shook as he brought down his gun, his face dark with disappointment. He could have booted himself for trying to show off. And before Hart, whom he admired more than any man except his father.

He looked at the scout. Hart's eyes were following two pinions out of the sky. He seemed not to notice Rod's discomfiture. When the feathers were out of sight among the trees, he turned to the boy:

"Better than good, Rod. You'll do!"

Soon Rod settled into the routine. He shared the small tent with Hart and John Fox, somewhat to the latter's annoyance. Like Hart, Rod continued to wear his own deerskin shirt and moccasins, to carry his own rifle. And, as Hart explained kindly, "We aren't actually in the Army—just attached."

John Fox found many a small chore for Rod to do, such as shining his boots, tightening the tent ropes, cleaning up, and finding bait for fishing, which was one of the few amusements available to the men at the fort. Rod did them all without protest. He had no grandiose ideas about his rank.

The other soldiers tried a mild sort of hazing. Some told him wild and improbable tales of military life, and guffawed when he believed them. Others sent him on foolish errands which ended nowhere. One fellow even stuffed Rod's coat pockets with conch shells while the young scout was swimming in the river. Some of the animals were decayed, so that for days Rod had to wear his summer homespun, while his leather jacket aired in a lonely spot near the woods' edge.

The boy was good-natured about it all, and soon the pranks ended, for lack of interest.

He and Hart had long talks, and the older man confided to Rod that he foresaw long trouble ahead. Although he knew the Indians' side of the argument too plainly for comfort and did not believe they should be forced to emigrate, he was stern in his thought that Florida must be defended from violence.

During the scout's many arguments with John Fox, Rod obtained a deeper understanding of Territorial problems, which was to help him in years ahead. He learned more about the Treaty of Fort Moultrie, made in 1823, which gave the Indians a reservation in the central part of the Territory and promised them they could live there for twenty years. Hart said it was the business of the white men to live up to their agreement, and John Fox agreed.

Fox said that it was the white settlers' hunger for land that brought about the Treaty of Payne's Landing, nine years later. This treaty, he said, ignored the "twenty years" mentioned in the first, and bound the Indians to move to Arkansas at once, where lands had been offered them. It was only after much grumbling that a number of chiefs signed the treaty, saying their bands would go if the land was suitable. They stipulated that they must first see Arkansas.

Rod already knew the next strange chapter in this story of strange treaties. A delegation of seven chiefs had visited Arkansas, accompanied by white men, and signed the Treaty of Fort Gibson, agreeing that every Indian in Florida would move. John Fox said the chiefs were drunk with white-man whiskey when they made their crosses on the fateful paper.

The Indians at home were angry because the chiefs had

igned. They had no right, these others said. The matter should be put to a vote of the nation. But a vote was refused.

At the last council of chiefs in the spring of 1835, Osceola had flung his knife into the pages of the agreement, crying, "This is the only way I will make a treaty!"

As Rod mulled over the matter in his mind, he agreed with the others, who felt that the original contract had been broken by the white men themselves. Like his father, Rod could not see any good reason for the war which loomed.

Rod and John Fox talked about other things, too—President Andrew Jackson's tempestuous term in the White House, and whether Martin Van Buren would be elected president in the fall.

Shakochee came to see Rod just once during that time. He was standing at the edge of the woods early one morning when Rod came out of his tent. Although the white boy motioned him to come closer, Shakochee did not move.

Rod walked across the clearing toward his friend. As he came near, he saw that Shakochee's face was serious above the red and black bear carving that hung from a thong around his neck. Not until the white boy halted before him did the Indian say, "I will not see you again."

The words were like a blow. "Why not?" faltered Rod.

"My uncle, in whose house I live, will not stay here. We go to another place."

The boys stared at each other. At last Rod burst out, "Let me talk to Hart Whitley! Maybe they could use you as a guide at the post."

Shakochee shook his head slowly. "I must go."

Still he did not move. Rod stood silent, too, not knowing what to say but reluctant to part with his friend. It seemed a terrible thing to sever ties so suddenly.

"I hope the carving will bring you luck," he said at last.

"It is a good charm," Shakochee murmured.

Abruptly, as he had done once before, the Seminole turned and ran lightly into the woods, without another word or backward look. Rod watched him until he was out of sight, then slowly walked back toward his tent. Although it weighed heavily upon him that his friendship with Shakochee must end so quickly, and that he might never see him again, he did not spend time grieving. He sensed dimly that he must be strong, that harder things might lie ahead, and that he must be ready for them.

So he joined his two tentmates with a gusty "Good morning!" and pitched into the work as if nothing at all had happened.

Shortly after the murder of Charley E-Mathlar, three hundred riflemen were ordered out and five hundred volunteers were summoned by Richard Keith Call, the governor. General Clinch, in charge of Florida's armies, sent a foolscap circular through two counties urging men to come to the frontier posts.

While the whites were making these preparations to fight, the Indians launched their first direct attack—at Wakahoota on the East Coast—burning a plantation and killing several white men. And when volunteer forces marched toward Fort Micanopy, in the center of the state, they were set upon savagely and forced to turn back.

Thus the war took shape and form. As a great forest fire starts first with a little spiral of smoke, eats its way across an area of dry brush and leaps into the trees, so the Seminole War in 1835 began with the murder of a chieftain, with calls to arms, the marching of troops and sporadic attacks by the Indians.

Hart Whitley was sent away on a mysterious mission, and Rod was the only remaining scout at the fort. The friendly Indians who had previously served as runners were afraid to venture away since the E-Mathlar murder.

Early one morning, a few days before Christmas, Major Belton called Rod to his desk and quizzed him about his knowledge of the country. After ten minutes of questions, he smiled.

"All right, boy—want to take a dispatch to Fort King?"

Excitement rose in Rod. "Yes, sir."

The officer watched him keenly. "It's an important communication. If it weren't, I'd make one of the Indians go."

"Yes, sir."

"You'll start in half an hour. Come back here at that time. I'll order a horse for you."

"Yes, sir." Rod saluted and returned to his tent. He spent the half hour getting provisions for himself and his mount and putting them in the saddlebags. Major Belton had sent him a tall swift black. Rod made friends with him, patted his nose and fed him a bit of corn, then went back to the tent for a last check up.

When the thirty minutes had passed, he again stood before Major Belton at the officer's desk. Belton held out a sliver of foolscap, folded lengthwise.

"It's best that you don't know what this says, Rod. It's in French so the Indians won't be able to read it, if they capture you. Where are you going to keep it?"

"In my cap, sir," said Rod, reaching for the paper.

Major Belton hesitated. "Your cap could be knocked into the river and you'd never recover it."

"That's right, sir." Rod puckered his brows and thought. At last he said, "How about sewing it to my shirt, sir? It couldn't get away from me then."

"All right."

The major dispatched an orderly to find some thread, and Rod solemnly sewed the foolscap in long stitches to his shirt, just inside the shoulder. When it was finished, he felt it from the outside.

"Hardly even makes a bump," he observed.

Major Belton nodded. "That'll be fine, Rod. Be sure to hand it to General Thompson yourself. Good luck."

Rod saluted and went outside to where his mount was waiting. He vaulted into the saddle, waved to several men who looked up as he passed, and rode out the gate along the military road.

He was tremendously excited, but steady. The message was important—Major Belton had said so. And the ride to Fort King was filled with danger for any lone traveler. He thought of the express rider who had been murdered last August. Should Rod meet hostile Indians that might be his fate, too.

Impatiently he spurred his horse through the sun-flecked hammock spreading back from the Hillsborough. This was his first real mission for the Army, and he resolved that he would carry it through—somehow.

The ride was long. The hammock changed to pineland, its ramrod growth relaxing into delicate featherwork against the blue sky of midmorning. Sharp-fronded dwarf palmettos crouched beneath the tall trees, their leaves rattling faintly in the wind. Occasionally Rod saw the velvety backs of brown deer bounding away, or glimpsed the brilliance of jays in flight. Through the beat of his horse's hoofs, he could hear the liquid call of the mocking bird or the dick-a-dee-da of the white-eyed vireo.

His emotions subsided as the sun rose high, pouring heat into the pinewoods. His horse slowed, and he did not rake it with his heels. At noon he reached into his saddlebags for a bit of hardbread and ate it in the saddle. Later he stopped at a small spring to rest the black and to drink. His impatience had simmered down now to a dogged resolve to carry through his job.

Early in the afternoon, he passed through a small hammock of live oak, where the road skirted a swampy area choked with lily pads. The sudden scolding of two squirrels made him draw rein.

For a second he could not decide what to do. Was that a warning that someone was coming along the trail? Should he guide his mount into the undergrowth? A panicky fear urged him to hide among the moss and shadows of the trees.

But he sat his horse, waiting. After a time, when no more warning sounds were heard, he moved ahead again. It would not do to get scared. He did not have time for hiding beside the trail while the bright afternoon slipped away. The message must be delivered.

Night had almost closed down when Rod halted and led his mount off the road into a thick growth of water oaks beside a stream. He gave the animal a few handfuls of corn and let it graze. Although the air was chilly, he did not build a fire, preferring safety to comfort. He was hungry enough to relish his cold food, and his body welcomed its bed on the ground.

He slept soundly, awoke in the grayness of early morning, and resumed his ride. Now he made excellent time, for his horse was fresh and willing to gallop in the cold air. They flew along the military road, filled with a sense of power and certainty that they could cope with any danger. But when the sun rose high again and bathed them in its heat, the horse slackened and the boy could get little speed out of him.

Again night came, and rest and dawn. In that way Rod traveled up the peninsula, through what had once been Indian reservation by the Treaty of Fort Moultrie, but now was claimed by white men.

As he moved northeast, the country became richer. Black-muck swamps, starred with white lilies, watered the heavy vegetation that grew along their banks. The number of streams and little lakes increased. There were fewer pine flats and more hammock, where live oaks, magnolias, gum trees and cabbage palms crowded together, each struggling to grow toward the life-giving sun.

As Rod approached a bend in the trail late one afternoon, half a day's ride from Fort King, he saw a horse and rider through the trees. Instantly he recognized Ruther's roan. And a second later he saw the black bulk of Dan'l astride a pony, following his master.

The boy drew rein sharply. His heart rose into his throat. He thought of what his father had said about Ruther. Would the man try to kill him?

In spite of Rod's fright, his mind was not idle. With a quick, strong pressure on the rein, he wheeled his horse full around, rode it back the trail a few feet and sent it plunging into an animal trail tangent to the main path.

Behind him he heard a shout. Ruther had seen.

Through tall grasses and sapling growth the little trail twisted, so narrow it almost faded into the brush at spots. Rod let his horse have its head, only gouging it with his heels to make it run.

He prayed that the trail would not run out. But even as the thought came, he faced disaster. Before him a fallen pine, a monster of the woods, lay directly across his path. Garlanded thickly with moss, its branches reached high to the left, an impenetrable forest. To the right, in the place where it had once cast its shadow, lay a pool of sunlight which had nourished a wiry stand of saplings. There was no hope of riding around the tree. Deer must have leaped it, but the log was high for a horse.

As Rod hesitated, the ugly crack of a rifle sounded and returned from the forest as a moaning echo. Rod felt a sharp stab of pain in the forearm.

With a quick gouge of his heels, he sent his mount hurtling forward, bending low over the animal's mane and giving him full rein. The fallen tree rose before them like a wall. Rod closed his eyes, felt himself rising. He looked, saw the forest rushing past and was almost unseated as his mount struck ground.

As the horse regained his stride and sped smoothly along the trail, Rod threw back his head and laughed in triumph. He had seemed trapped a moment before—now he was free. He patted the animal fondly and praised him for the jump. And his heart warmed to Major Belton because the man had given him such a fine mount.

Half a mile beyond the tree, he stole a glance backward. No one was in sight, and the sun-flecked forest was quiet. For caution's sake he went another mile, then halted beside a moss-grown hammock. Still feeling that he should hide himself more thoroughly, he dismounted and led the horse through a thicket, parting the branches for him to follow. When at last they were deep within its shadow, Rod dropped his rein over a branch and turned to his wound.

The sight of it, when he rolled back his sleeve, scared him. A muscle oozed laxly from the hole and over it poured a stream of blood, spattering the black dirt and ferns with red. He sat down on the ground, leaned against the prickly fans of a cabbage palm and held up his arm to stop the flow, wondering why he hadn't realized this was a bad wound. But he could not hold his arm high for long. The woods began to turn black around him. A tarnish came over the sunshine. He threw himself flat on the ground, trying not to lose consciousness. And suddenly the thought that Ruther actually had tried to kill him rolled over his mind in a tidal wave of terror.

He lay there for a long time. When he roused, it was turning dark. The air was chilly, and a remote white moon was shining down into his hiding spot. His horse was still standing near.

He sat up cautiously, tenderly touched the flesh around his wound. Although blood still was oozing from the hole, it was just a trickle. His arm was covered with sticky, drying fluid.

He rolled down the sleeve of the hunting jacket, covering the bullet hole, and tried to rise. At first he was dizzy. But gradually, as he stood there, clinging to a pine trunk, his head cleared. Close above him a big owl whirred through the treetops, and far off he heard the wailing howl of a wolf.

More than anything, he would have liked to stay here until morning. He thought how good it would feel to lie down again and sleep. He thought, too, about the danger of wandering off the road at night, in some pine barren where the trail was dim.

These arguments he weighed against another—he had a message to deliver. It should have reached the post by now. A grown man would go on, he thought.

He stood up, fumbled for his horse's rein and led it back to the trail. There he mounted and took the road for Fort King.

For a time he was all right, then his dizziness returned. The star-sprinkled sky wheeled toward the black earth, and the forest faded into an undulating dark curtain. He leaned forward, hanging onto his mount's neck, and let the animal find its own way.

All through the late night hours he kept on, scarcely knowing where he went, but pushing ahead. And in the first gray light of morning he came to a clearing. The log buildings of the fort loomed ahead. There was a fire in the nearest cabin and a hazy pinkish wisp of smoke rising out of the chimney.

He stopped there, knocked. As he waited for someone to answer, he leaned weakly against the logs of the building. Although he felt very sick, he was proud. He had completed his mission.

Chapter III

Attack

"The murder of General Thompson and Lieutenant
Smith was not known until some hours after, but
the fate of Rogers was announced by the smoke
and flames of his dwelling, which now arose far
above the dense hammock which surrounded it."

—JOHN T. SPRAGUE
in *The Florida War,* 1848

Erastus Rogers, sutler at Fort King, welcomed Rod into the
house and sat him down before the fire. The sutler was a
hearty, brisk-mannered man, who wore the buckskins of a
woodsman but had filled his cabin with many of the furnishings
of civilization. Fine mahogany chairs with cushioned seats sat
beside the homemade hide-bottoms of the frontier, and a hand-
some crystal chandelier, fitted with candles, hung from the
center of the room.

The man gestured toward Rod's wound. "Looks as if somebody wanted you dead," he observed, with a trace of indignation.

"Yes."

Rogers' tone was kind. "We'll fix it up in a hurry."

He brought in a box of torn bandages and a pan of hot
water, and set them on the hearth in front of Rod.

"Not yet," said the boy stubbornly. "I've a message for General Thompson and I'll deliver it first."

But when he tried to rise, Rogers eased him back into the chair.

"Now you make up your mind to stay there for a while," he coaxed. "I'll send my colored boy down with the note."

Rod shook his head. "I promised Major Belton I'd hand it to the general."

"Too bad," clucked the sympathetic sutler. "It would be perfectly safe and would reach the general in just a few minutes. Want me to take it myself?"

Rod shook his head again. "I'll be fine in a minute. I'll go."

The sutler eyed him gravely, as if doubting his words. "I'll get you some strong tea," he offered. "That'll brace you."

He hurried into the kitchen and in a few minutes returned with a steaming mugful of the brew.

"There now. Try that."

"Thank you, sir."

Rod sipped the tea slowly. It did seem to bring back his energy, bit by bit, and he was grateful for its warmth. While he drank, Rogers poked up the fire and fed it a new log. Rod was looking into the sutler's trading post, where already a clerk was opening the doors and letting the morning sun shine across bolts of cloth, beads, shirts, guns and powder, liquor, groceries, and nearly every commodity wanted on the frontier.

Rogers sank into a chair and waited for the log to catch. As his eyes flicked across Rod, they paused at the throat of the boy's hunting shirt.

"What's that—around your neck?"

Rod tried to conceal his pride as he drew out his new eagle charm. "It's one of my carvings," he explained. "I wear it for luck."

Rogers examined it closely. "Shows a lot of skill. That cruel beak is mighty realistic."

"Thank you, sir."

"Think you could do some more of these things?"

"I do them all the time, sir. The soldiers and Indians at Fort Brooke use them for lucky pieces. One of them stopped a bullet last year."

The sutler's eyes widened. "Lucky the fellow who was wearing that one! And I'll bet your carvings have a reputation." He paused, stared absently out of the window and said abruptly, "Look, I'll buy as many of those charms as you can make while you're here—and let you eat at my table, too. My cook, Effie, is the best within five hundred miles, so that's an offer worth accepting. Is it a bargain?"

Rod hesitated, pleased but uncertain. "I didn't intend staying here, sir. But if I do have to wait for a message to take back, I'll be glad to make some carvings."

"Fine. More tea?"

"No, thanks, sir. I've got to deliver the message now."

Rod set down his cup. But before he could rise there were footsteps on the path outside. The door opened and a broad-shouldered officer entered, his gold epaulettes gleaming in the light of the morning sun. He was followed by a young lieutenant.

"Good morning, Rogers," said the officer briskly. "This the lad?"

Rogers advanced with a cordial "Good morning, General Thompson! And Lieutenant Smith! The young man here was just insisting on going down to the fort. A little strong tea has stiffened his legs, and he thought he could walk it."

Rod was taken aback at the sudden appearance of the Indian agent himself, but the general's next words offered an explanation.

"Thanks for sending word, Rogers. It's just as well to talk with him up here."

Rod was already on his feet and saluting. He flashed a grateful smile toward the sutler as he reached into his shirt, ripped loose the message and handed it to General Thompson.

"I'd have been down to the fort myself, sir, in another minute."

"Never mind," said the general kindly. "The important thing was to get it here from Fort Brooke."

He read the dispatch, stared at it silently for a moment, then stuffed it into his inside coat pocket. Turning to the sutler, he asked briskly, "Where's that flour you promised us? You said it left Picolata weeks ago. We're running low."

"I'm expecting it any day, sir," replied Rogers quickly.

"Well, don't forget, we're going to need it desperately inside of eight or ten days."

"Yes, sir. I'll see that you have it."

General Thompson turned to Rod. "I'll have a dispatch for you to take back—if you're able—day after tomorrow."

"I'll be ready, sir."

The general nodded to the sutler, turned and went out the door, a little absently, as if he were thinking about the contents of the message.

"There, that's settled," observed Rogers, with satisfaction. "Now, Rod, can you eat some breakfast?"

"Not much, sir. If I could have a good drink of water, I think I'd like to sleep now."

"Fine."

He brought Rod a dipperful of clear spring water, then took him into a lean-to off the main building and pointed to a carved walnut bed.

"Best bed in the house, Rod. I had it shipped all the way from Rhode Island and carted across from Volusia. Make yourself comfortable."

"Thanks, sir."

"If you're not up before dinnertime, I'll wake you. I want you to get a good meal before night. There's part of a Christmas turkey left over, and some pork and pheasant."

"Christmas?" faltered Rod. "When . . ."

"Yesterday," said Rogers cheerfully. "Didn't you know?"

"No," said Rod dully. "I—guess I lost track."

"Too bad," clucked the sutler. "If you'd made it a day sooner you'd have shared my Christmas morning eggnog. There was a crowd around here all day long, cutting up and drinking nog. Well, so long, Rod. I'll call you for dinner."

Rod lay down on the bed. There was a vague aching inside him at having missed Christmas, with its bright warmth and jolly memories. He wondered if there were gifts for him at home and realized suddenly that in his absorption with his new life, he had prepared no gifts for his family. That thought hurt, too, until he remembered that Rogers had ordered some carvings. He could trade them for something at the store— get a present for each one of the Wheelers.

Having delivered his message and planned something for tomorrow, he dropped off to sleep in a few seconds, forgetting, with human inconsistency, the creeping conflagration that burned brighter and brighter in the deep forests of the Territory.

After two days at Fort King, Rod was ready to return to Fort Brooke with General Thompson's message. His wound was healing quickly, Effie's good meals had put an extra pound or two on him, and he had traded several lucky pieces for presents he would take back to his family.

When he hadn't been carving, he had mingled with the fifty or so soldiers stationed at the frontier fort or talked with the friendly Indians camped close by, most of whom seemed afraid to leave the garrison since the shooting of Charley E-Mathlar.

One old Indian, Henry Tall Boy, told of trails to Picolata and Volusia, settlements on the way to the East Coast. Rod tried to memorize them, and at night, in the sutler's, he drew pictures of them. If he was to be a messenger and guide, he must know the country.

On December twenty-eighth, he called to see General Thompson, but was told the general's message was not yet ready, to come back the next day.

Rod wandered back to the sutler's and spent the afternoon carving new charms and watching Effie bake dried-apple pies for dinner. From the cabin he could see several of the fort's soldiers digging a ditch outside the pickets of the stockade. He wished his arm were well, so he could offer to help them, for he knew that many of the small garrison were ill with measles.

Rogers had a guest for the evening meal—a Mr. LaRue of St. Augustine, a land promoter who was scanning the reservation in expectation of buying land when the Seminoles moved west. He was a smooth-mannered, elegantly dressed individual with oily black hair and a great confidence in his own plans.

When LaRue and the quiet store clerk, James Condon, were seated at the dinner table with Rod and the sutler, LaRue launched into a prophecy concerning the Seminole War. It would be over very swiftly, he said. There were not more than five or six hundred warriors in the Territory. General Clinch had many more fighters in the field already, counting both regulars and volunteer troops. In addition, fourteen companies in border states stood ready to serve in the Florida campaign.

"A good fight or two and the Indians will go to Arkansas— and in a hurry," he concluded, helping himself to one of Effie's corn cakes.

Forgetting his youth, Rod spoke up: "There's lots more warriors than that, Mr. LaRue. And Hart Whitley says they'll never be caught in one army. He thinks . . ."

He was interrupted by a laugh from LaRue. "Suppose there are even as many as a thousand warriors. Less than half of them want to fight. The others want to go west. What happens? We deal a heavy blow to the cocky ones—like Osceola— and poof! His prestige is gone. The others will come in and

we can ship them off to New Orleans. That will leave a handful to deal with, and they'll probably sneak off south to the
swamps."

Rod said nothing. He wondered if the man could be right.
LaRue had traveled a lot and knew influential people. Maybe
he had more information than Hart Whitley.

LaRue was speaking again. This time Rod did not listen.
Through the man's talk he heard a faint sound. Ears alert, he
listened. It came again—close. He could not tell if it was a
footstep or merely the swish of wind in the leaves.

Something of his strained attitude communicated itself.
"What's the matter?" asked Rogers.

Rod smiled, shamefaced. "Guess I'm jumpy. I thought I
heard someone outside."

Rogers pushed back his chair. "It's General Thompson—
he was coming here. He and Lieutenant Smith . . ."

He was interrupted by a blood-chilling war whoop that
pierced the quiet house like a hurricane wind and echoed in
the far woods.

"Indians!" cried LaRue, his face white.

Rifles thundered close by, drowning the sutler's reply. An
instant later, the glass in the windows shattered and fell, to
break again with a tinkle as it hit the floor. Then suddenly the
air was alive with bullets glancing above the table and thudding
into the log walls. With a sharp click, the gravy dish broke
and partridge gravy whipped across the cloth.

There was a scream of terror from Effie in the kitchen, followed by silence.

The dinner guests jumped to their feet. Elbowing one another, tipping over chairs, they scrambled to get away. Rod
slipped quietly under the long board, hand on his knife. He
berated himself for having left his rifle in the small room lent
him by the sutler. His belt gun was there, too, on the floor beside
the carved bed.

Scuttling along the floor, he moved toward the room. The others had crowded toward the back of the house, but he paid no attention. He must have his guns.

In the small room, he found his pistol and stuck it into his belt. The rifle lay across a washstand, beside his powder horn and shot pouch. He stood up cautiously, hung the ammunition containers over his shoulders and picked up the gun. Armed, he felt better.

Rifles were battering at the door of the cabin, and through the entrance to the store, Rod glimpsed naked bodies in the light of flickering torches. He ran out of the small room, dodged past the littered table and into the kitchen.

There he stopped. Blows rained against the barred back door. He halted in panic, uncertain where to turn. As he did so, the front door crashed in and he heard a wild war whoop of triumph.

A whisper came to him—so soft that he hardly believed it was real. "Boy!"

He looked around and saw no one. Again the single word came, its strong insistence carrying above the din outside. Rod's gaze flicked to the little storage shed just off the kitchen. Effie was peeking from behind a barrel, beckoning to him, so scared the whites of her eyes were like signals in the dimness of the place.

Rod stepped softly into the shed and crouched behind a barrel next to Effie's. "Where are the others?" he whispered.

"Gone." Her voice was trembling.

"To the fort?"

"South, Master Rod. But hush now."

Footsteps were streaming through the house, coming in the back door. Torches lighted the dusky space behind the barrels, but no one came into the storeroom. Everywhere the war whoop resounded vigorously, edged with the crazed jubilance of victory.

Suddenly the Indians were gone. The house seemed very still, except for an ominous crackling. Off to the south, where Rogers and the others had sought safety, the night was a-quaver with war cries. In the hammock rifles sounded.

Effie moaned. "God a-mercy! They's caught 'em!"

"Be still!" cautioned Rod.

Someone was entering the cabin. A faint creak of hinges—a mere fragment of sound in the reverberating night. Another creak—the floor. The soft buckskin of moccasins brushing against the roughly planed logs.

Slowly the sound came nearer. It paused at all the rooms, advanced to the back of the house, hesitated at the door to the storeroom.

Rod crouched, rigid, hand on his belt gun. Through a tiny slit between the two barrels he could see into the kitchen. It was lighted by the soft glow of pitch pine in the hearth and by a torch held overhead. On the threshold, carrying a flaming pine stick, stood a tall Indian.

He was all but naked, his body painted red. He wore a long calico shirt and carried a powder horn and shot pouch slung over a shoulder. In one hand he gripped a flintlock rifle, mounted in gleaming silver. His face was extraordinary—mouth arched upward almost in a smile, forehead somewhat receding, but high and noble, powerful nose down-curving. In his brightly printed turban he wore tafa luste—the black plumes of the Mikasukies and Seminoles. Several dried scalps hung from his belt.

Although he had never before seen this Indian, Rod knew him at once as the rebel leader, Osceola. The silver-mounted rifle alone would have identified the brave, for didn't everyone know that General Thompson had given Osceola such a rifle in an attempt to win his friendship?

The boy held his breath while Osceola looked around the room. A slow contortion swept across the proud face, and in it Rod seemed to see the essence of all Indian hatreds. Seizing a table with one hand, the warrior sent it careening across the kitchen to sprawl on the hearth, one leg in the fire. The torch came down to ignite a basket woven of rushes, which stood beside the mantel.

Then, with a final, dramatic sweep, Osceola raked his blazing stick across the herbs that hung drying from the ceiling rafters and laughed as the thatch on the roof caught fire and sent out a quick cloud of smoke.

He was gone. Again the house was still, except for the crackling of the flames. The war whoops sounded far off, in the hammock.

Rod jumped up. "Effie! Hurry!"

But already Effie was squeezing out from behind the other barrel. Holding her skirts up, she ran toward the front of the house. Rod followed. The door stood open, sagging on its hinges. Outside, dusk had begun to creep over the clearing.

At the door Effie paused, not knowing which way to run. Rod glanced toward the hammock. It was nearer, but he had heard rifle shots there, and shouts. No one could tell what lay within its darkness.

"The fort!" he urged.

They turned that way, running madly across the clearing toward the stockade, dodging the few trees that still stood between the fort and the post.

Z-zing!

A bullet burned past them, ground to powder a bit of oak bark. Again the deep groan of a rifle, its bullet slashing the oak leaves.

Effie stumbled, screaming. Rod jerked her up. They ran again. It seemed like hours. Slowly the stockade came closer. The big gate was opening. Someone had seen them.

Then they were inside.

Chapter IV

Dade's Men

"Within the triangle, along the north and west faces of it, were about thirty bodies. . . . These were lying, almost every one of them, in precisely the position they must have occupied during the fight. . . ."

—Captain E. A. Hitchcock's official report of Dade's battleground

Three days later, between sunset and moonrise, the stockade gate opened again. Rod slipped through it, quietly.

It was the third time the huge log door had been unbarred since Rod and Effie had come through it. The first was when four soldiers had brought in the bodies of General Thompson and Lieutenant Smith. The two officers were found on the hill, along the road to the sutler's home. Both had been shot many times and scalped. The gate had been opened again, at night, when the two were buried.

Although volunteers had gone into the hammock to search for the bodies of the good-natured sutler and the land promoter, LaRue, no trace of them was found, and an Indian attack had cut short the hunt. James Condon, the clerk, who had left the house with them, had chosen to run toward the stockade. He escaped with a minor bullet wound and now spent most of his time glaring fiercely over a rifle toward the hammock, hoping to sight a Seminole.

Ever since the first attack, Indians had laid close siege to the fort, knowing it manned by a handful of soldiers. They hid in the hammock around it, shouting their war whoops, yelling taunts and sniping whenever a soldier showed himself. Twice they charged—at night and early in the morning—and in the excitement of returning their fire the fort's supply of ammunition was brought dangerously low.

The men inside the stockade took turns at the loopholes, picking off any warrior unwise enough to show himself within rifle range. They were heartened by the knowledge that Major Dade's company—over a hundred men—was due from Fort Brooke to reinforce them.

Effie had suffered hysteria after reaching the fort, but soon recovered enough to take over the cooking chores. She was less scared, she confided to Rod, when she was standing over the fire with a skillet in her hand. So a man was freed to fight, and many of them said the victuals were better than before, even though Effie had only the Army's pork and flour and beans with which to work.

On the third day the Indians seemed to have withdrawn. The commanding officer asked for volunteers to take a message to Fort Drane and had given Rod a return mission to Fort Brooke.

"Dade's force should be here any hour now. When you meet them on the way, tell them we're in desperate circumstances."

Rod was glad to go. A siege wasn't to his taste. He would have liked to ride, but the Indians had stolen his fine horse; besides, going afoot was safer now, the commander said.

The air was cold, the stars bright. Once out of the big gate, Rod eased into a bit of oak thicket and waited, hands clutching his rifle. Beyond the crest of the slope which led to the sutler's store, he could see in vague outline the rock chimney, rising like an Indian sacrificial pole out of the burned ruins of the building. Still farther west, concealed by the hill, was the blackness of the hammock.

There were no close, reassuring night sounds. Rifle thunder and fire had frightened away the woods creatures. Only from far off in the pine country sounded the howl of wolves.

To the north, somewhere near the trail to Fort Drane, Rod saw a reddish, smoke-laden column rising into the night sky, dimming the stars around it. That could be no one but Indians. He was glad his mission wasn't to Fort Drane.

He chose a clump of scrub oak part way up the hill and moved toward it, treading lightly so as not to snap a twig or send an echo through the earth. The soft buckskin of his moccasins enabled him to feel the ground before he trusted his weight to it.

He gained the clump, a little breathless, and waited again before going on. Nothing happened. The clearing was still. He chose another low oak and walked cautiously toward it.

Near the crest of the hill he began to move in a wide semi-circle around the sutler's burned home. He could not say why he did this. It was his instinct to stay away from the charred logs of the former store.

As he moved beyond the ruin, he could see the cleared path of the military road, where it meandered across the clearing and was swallowed up in the black hammock. To the left was the spot where the friendly Indians had camped. It was deserted.

He had a strong distaste for the military road. It would be watched closely by Indians—that he knew. Also, it was near there that Rogers and his guest had disappeared. Their bodies might still lie beneath the trees. As such a place he feared it.

But he reminded himself that the road was the best way to Fort Brooke, and the only trail he could travel at night. Without wavering he moved in its direction.

As he neared the dark growth of the oaks, he slowed, waiting behind each tree to see if the path was clear, flitting from dense palmetto clump to shielding mantle of wild grapevine, keeping within deep shadow wherever he could. At each pause he listened, waited. When he was satisfied that no one stalked him, he pushed ahead.

It was slow going, but at last he reached the hammock. Still he was cautious. Staying to one side of the road, he continued his jerky advance—hiding and listening, moving quickly forward, hiding once more.

When he was a mile into the woods, he began to feel reassured. The night sounds were breaking out around him: The sleepy twittering of a bird aroused from its night rest, the shrill purring of a tree frog, the three-noted shout of the whippoorwills. At one of his halts, a lumbering possum scared him so badly that his knees turned weak. But he smiled to himself when the animal had gone past. This was a good omen, for it meant that the forest close around did not hold an encampment of Indians.

When the moon rose, he was several miles from Fort King, stepping more quickly now, but hanging close to the blotchy shadows of the tall pines. Still alert, still listening sharply for any sound, he walked without pausing.

Miles reeled away under his moccasined feet. The winter stars wheeled over the moon-whitened swathe cut by the military road. When the sky brightened to the east, Rod found suddenly that he was tired. He began to look for a thick hammock, where he could hide and rest during the day.

But the hammocks were infrequent here. He walked a long way and did not find one. At last he chose a thick clump of palmettos growing beneath a forest of pines. He curled up under the sheltering fans and promptly went to sleep.

He woke to find the noon sun beating down on his little refuge, and his clothes damp with sweat. Peering out, he saw a broad stretch of pineland which offered little concealment.

After a careful look around, he boldly walked back to the

road and again paced along it, holding his rifle in both hands, ready to fling it to his shoulder. Once the pounding of a deer herd frightened him and he ducked beneath the scrub. When the deer had gone he came out, looking sheepish, and again moved along the trail.

It was midafternoon when he noticed the buzzards. They were still a long way ahead, wheeling thickly over the road. Rod had never seen so many.

The sight of them was like a cold stone laid against the bare pit of his stomach. It was always that way. For to Rod, buzzards meant death.

Maybe they were eating a dead deer, or a lost calf—that was usually the reason for a flock of the ugly, bald-headed birds.

He stopped, watched them a moment as they circled, inky-black and glistening against the bright blue of the sky.

They were at something, he knew that for sure. Something dead and unguarded. Whatever it was, it could no longer hurt him, or the buzzards would not be there.

He forced himself to keep on, feeling a dread that was beyond his natural abhorrence. To combat it, he told himself this was only one of those everyday happenings in the woods— a dead bear, or deer, or wolf—maybe a stray cow, or even a horse.

When he was still some distance away from the birds, he noticed a strange and foreign object. It appeared to be a high log fence, right in the middle of the road. He could not believe his eyes, for there was no dwelling between Tampa and Fort King.

Shading his eyes, he stopped in the road and stared. He saw that it was not a fence but a wall, forming an obtuse angle on the trail. A breastwork—or part of one. That's what it was. As if a lot of men—or an army . . .

With a shock of relief he remembered Major Dade's company—expected at Fort King. It would have come along this road. It had been attacked by Indians and the men had fortified themselves at this spot.

All his oppressive fear slid away in an instant. The thought of shelter for himself and reinforcements for Fort King filled him with happy excitement. He opened his mouth to shout, but checked the impulse immediately. They wouldn't know who he was. Someone might shoot.

A flag—a white flag—that's what he needed. That would let him walk ahead safely. He wore nothing white, but he peeled off his buckskin coat and the faded blue homespun shirt he wore next his skin. The shirt made an acceptable flag, he thought.

Heart thumping, Rod walked forward slowly, holding the garment above him, and moving it back and forth sometimes, so it would fan out and be seen. Surely anyone would honor a flag of this sort—at least long enough to see what its bearer wanted.

There was a frightening two or three minutes, when his heart seemed to be coming up into his throat. It would be so easy to shoot him. He was a broad target, walking up to the breastwork.

As he drew near, he became conscious that the buzzards hovered close overhead. They were like a dark cloud between the fort and the sun. The gasping beat of their wings filled the air. Some of them settled outside the timbers. But the others—he halted when he saw—came down inside the logs.

Trembling, he advanced again. Strange that no one shouted to him.

"Hello!" he called.

His own voice came back from the pines.

He was close now, close enough to see how carelessly the breastwork was constructed. At one corner three of the logs were toppling inward. And suddenly he almost stumbled over a cluster of dead bodies clad in uniforms of the United States Army.

Fear gripped him, and he ran forward, shouting. No answer came. He saw guns pointing at him through the logs, but none fired. He reached the breastwork and sped along its wall. Buzzards flew up, rising with slow reluctance.

There was no opening in the barricade. He kept on running. He jumped across a dead man, ran around the side of the fort. There must be a gate somewhere.

The back of the breastwork was open, showing the whole inside of the defense. Rod stood gazing, eyes fixed, unbelieving. Men stood along the wall, pointing their rifles through its wide spaces. Men lay on the ground. Men hung across the top of the logs. Lots of men—the core of Dade's company. Not one of them moved. They were dead.

Inside the fort was a small cannon. Several round shot were heaped close by, ready to load. The gunner lay crumpled beside his weapon, a cannon ball still clutched within the lifeless circle of his arms.

Rod turned away. Hardly knowing what he did, he ran west along the military road, forgetting caution, forgetting Indians, forgetting everything in the deep consciousness of disaster.

For a long time he ran, his legs powered by his terror. At last his good sense began to return. It told him to leave the road and go more cautiously. He did so. But his thoughts were not rational ones. He scarcely saw the woods and the objects around him. In his mind was a deep-burned picture of the dead men defending the fort. In his ears there rang the strong beat of buzzard's wings.

Chapter V

White-feathered Arrow

"Be it resolved . . . that the President of the United
States . . . cause rations to be delivered from the
public stores to the unfortunate sufferers who have
been driven from their homes by Indian depreda-
tions in Florida."

—Law passed by Congress
on February 1, 1836

Fort Brooke was making ready for attack. The two hundred
regulars stationed there were extending the stockades, moulding
bullets and laying in provisions in case of siege.

Almost every day, two or three wagonloads of settlers
bumped over the military road to the fort from little farms a
short distance inland. Some of them came down-river or along
the coast in small boats. All wanted the protection of the
garrison.

Many of these families stayed with Tampa friends, helping
them to build stockades around their homes and fit them with
loopholes for rifles. Others halted their wagons in shady spots
along the Hillsborough and slept and ate in the open, guns
handy.

Quite as eager for protection as the white families were the
friendly Indians, who camped near the Army post, offering
their services as scouts and messengers, or as fighters if war
came to the settlement on the bay.

News of the Dade massacre had reached Fort Brooke soon after the slaughter. Two survivors came in to tell their story of a death that struck suddenly along the trail, killing more than half the company in the first attack. They related how the remaining men had hastened to build a triangular breastwork, only to be fired on a second time before the logs were all in place. Private Clark, badly wounded, had lain among the dead bodies until darkness allowed him to escape. He reported there were no other survivors.

Rod saw again the log walls manned by dead men, and the same shock came back to him. This kind of killing was savagery. He had seen it himself and he knew. Hart was not now at the fort, and his slow, careful evaluation of men and events was missing. So Rod joined the others in their indignation and began calling the Indians "savages."

John Fox alone offered an abstract view. "Indians are raised to ignore pain," he said. "They're taught to hold a burning coal on their wrists when they're still boys, and it's the weak one that yells. So don't expect any quarter in a war with them."

Although Rod still lived at the fort, he visited his family often. They were staying with their relatives at Tampa, in a house that faced the bay, and Hugh was helping his Uncle Ace build a stockade across the rear of the property. Rod's father had ridden back to the Wheeler cabin to bring in a few things that had been left behind and to board up the home till the war was over.

Rod noticed that his mother's face grew worried as Mr. Wheeler's trip lengthened from four to six to eight days. At last she drew Rod aside in the storeroom of the house.

"Your father's been gone too long, Rod. It's nine days tomorrow. He didn't plan to stay any such time."

Rod understood without more words. "I'll go out there, Ma."

She looked relieved. "I was hoping you would." She prepared

a sack of food for him and saw him off, on Uncle Ace's small Indian pony.

The day was cool and he made good time along the trail. He had not been home—at least to the cabin that had always been home—for five weeks, and the landmarks near it smote him with poignant familiarity. He had treed a possum here, trapped a turtle there, killed a rattler once in this palmetto stretch.

At last he came to the cabin, and stood a minute staring at its boarded-up windows and weed-grown garden. It was hard to face the thought that this place was no longer his dwelling and that the house would remain here alone, defenseless against Indian looting.

He tried the front door, found it locked. Probably his father had barred it from the inside. He walked around to the back. That door was open. Rod pushed it wide and went in, half expecting to find his father there.

The main room was empty. It was the same, but shorn of many treasures. The spinning wheel was gone, and the pewter pans that had hung against the chimney. Ma's silver porringers no longer winked brightly from the little dish cabinet near by.

But the pull-down bed stood against the wall, and there was the ladder to the loft, up which he and Hughie and Dovvy had climbed after supper each night. And the table board with its long benches still was beside the hearth. It seemed like home, in spite of its deserted air.

"Pa!" he called.

He walked across the room and looked into the small lean-to that served as a storage shed. It was almost empty, for the Wheelers had taken their stores to Tampa, to share with Uncle Ace's family.

Uneasy, but still expecting to find his father, Rod went out the back door and around to the milkshed. It was empty. The cattle, too, had been taken in to Tampa, but Rod had hoped to find his father's horse here.

His alarm increased. There were no other buildings where his father might be—nothing else on the farm big enough to conceal a man.

He left the milkshed and set out across the pasture, following the edge of the property around their cornfield and skirting the rows of dead cotton. Now he was scared.

When he was nearly back to the grove, he stopped, cupped his hands and called, "Pa!"

A dismal, far-off echo repeated "Pa!"

"Pa!" he called again. "Pa!"

He stood there, calling, for long minutes. Sometimes he called before the echo had died, and his own voice jangled with the woods sound. Once he was silent for a time, thinking he caught an answer. Then, as a plump little dove under a palmetto repeated its throaty call, he heaved a clod of dirt at it, knowing it was the dove-note he had heard.

He walked on, a lost feeling spreading through him. But suddenly he had the thought that his father might be out hunting. He might have ridden a distance to find game. Maybe Uncle Ace had asked him to bring in something. There were lots of people camped around the fort now—game was getting scarce. It might well be that Pa had gone into the woods for a deer, or a sackful of partridges.

The fact that his father's horse was missing supported this theory, and Rod went back to the cabin, comforted.

Inside the house, he took another look around. It was clear that his father had not completed the job of packing. An extra shovel and an old hoe lay tied together in the middle of the floor, and a deer hide had been stacked on top of them. The hearth was filled with soft gray wood ashes.

Rod stepped toward it, leaned down, and felt of the ashes. They were cold. He had expected that, although he hoped they might surprise him. But as his eye flicked across the hearth, he noticed a small pot, set as if it had been left there to keep warm.

He picked it up, removed the cover and looked inside. Possum stew. The fetid smell told him it was several days old.

Rod's breath came fast. His father had not been back to the cabin for several days. He had expected to come back to the next meal, to eat the stew. Something had happened. There wasn't any doubt now.

Without pausing to plan, Rod went out to his pony, vaulted into the saddle and headed toward his father's favorite hunting ground.

Two miles east, he turned off along a deer path and rode toward the creek that ran through their property. This was wildwood—heavy growths of pine, oak, gum, cherry and the pungent bay were interwoven with grape, woodbine and climbing ivy. Only the dim trail led through it, turning and twisting, sometimes almost obscured. Rod followed it slowly, looking right and left wherever the woods broke and calling every so often, but getting no answer.

Where the tangle was thickest, he suddenly emerged upon a creek bank. Just below him the little stream widened, and there were marks of animals around it, as if the spot had long been used for a water hole.

At the creek edge, Rod looked for footprints. But he could see only the cloven marks of deer, the pads of a panther, and the many small-fingered paw patterns of raccoon.

Without pausing long, he plunged back into the woods, following a new animal trail. Carefully he scanned the path where it was sandy or damp. Again he found deer prints—lots of them. And suddenly his pulse beat hard inside his temples, for there, at the edge of the lightly trodden way, was the heel of a man's moccasin, faintly outlined over a dirt carving of a deer's hoof.

He hurried forward, excited over his small victory and confident that he would find his father soon.

Again he saw the moccasin imprint and recognized his

father's square-shaped foot. Where the trail grew muddy at the margin of a swamp, he paused eagerly before the tracks of both feet, walking with his father's long stride, toeing in a bit, just as he had seen them in the ploughed fields many times.

Rod stopped then and called. He called until the woods rang. But no answer came and fear stole over him once more. Could these tracks have been made yesterday, or earlier? At once he knew they were that old, or older. He examined them closely, found a bit of dry, crumbled earth in the heel of one and birds' tracks moving across another. Yes, his father had been here, but not today.

Disappointed, he stood up. The sense of loss hovered close, waiting to descend. He was afraid he could not follow his father through the long journey of a day or two.

He moved on, not expecting success, but keeping to the trail because there was nothing else to do. Where the path disappeared, he searched again until he picked it up. At last he lost it altogether.

He sat down on a log, discouraged but trying hard not to give up. His father had been here. He had not returned home. Something had happened. He must find out what it was.

At last he stood up. He did not know where to look. There were no footprints now—only the dim tree-crowded hammock, warmed by the afternoon sun and smelling of green ferns, vine and leaf mould. Surely, if his father were here, he would have heard Rod's call.

Judging his position by the late sun, the boy turned back toward the creek, cutting straight through the deepest part of the woods. Soon darkness would make him give up his hunt. He must hurry.

The windfall here was exceptionally thick, as if a hurricane center had moved across this part of the woods. Rod came to a huge tree, uprooted and half fallen, but wedged between two smaller trees that held it above ground. Underneath it the brush had flourished, fed by the sun that poured into this forest hole.

He reached high, clasped the tree trunk and vaulted up. There he stopped, staring. His eyes clung to something alien to the forest, while a harsh pain ran through him.

Beneath him an arrow shaft rose into the air, its white feathers gleaming like an exotic flower. The arrow point was buried in a man's buckskin-clad shoulder. Blood, dried and dark, had run out of the wound and down onto Will Wheeler's strong, sun-browned face that was grayish-yellow now, its features still as death.

For long seconds Rod could not move. Then he clambered down from the log and knelt beside the body. A strange, choked sound came out of his throat, but he did not hear it. He touched his father's hand, found it cold. He reached inside the hunting shirt to see if the heart was beating.

There was a faint pulsation. He rubbed the skin around the heart and chafed the wrists with desperate haste. When he felt for the heartbeat again, it seemed stronger.

He drew out his knife and, gritting his teeth, cut off the arrow where it entered the flesh. Those white-feathered arrows he remembered well. Next he cut oak branches, lashed them together with tough pieces of grapevine and rigged up a crude travois. With much tugging he moved his father's heavy body onto it, tying it on with more vine.

Between tasks, he listened to the flagging heart, rubbed the body around it, and urged his father to speak. He could not rouse him. Except for a groan when the body was moved onto the travois, there was no response.

It was almost dark when he finished, and Rod felt the night chill pierce his buckskins. Before starting home, he took off his jacket and laid it carefully across the wounded man. Then he moved slowly back toward the trail, trampling down brush and saplings in a broad swath until he reached the main path.

Night had come when he turned in at the farm. He eased
the travois through the front door, pulled it carefully to a spot
before the hearth, and set to work building a fire. As the flames
crackled up around the quick-burning pitch pine, he unbound
his father from the boughs, loosened the buckskin coat and examined the arrow wound. It was bleeding a bit from the rough
journey, but he had nothing with which to dress it. He turned
the puncture upward to check the blood flow and wondered, in
a panicky confusion of thoughts, what he should do next. He
would have given a lot if his mother had been there, for he
himself had no experience with wounds.

Although he knew she had taken all the medicines and clean
old rags which she used as bandages, he went to her cupboard
and looked inside. The shelves were empty, as he expected—but
his eyes lighted at sight of one tall bottle. On the highest board,
out of reach of small hands, was his mother's supply of bitters.
In the excitement of leaving, she had forgotten to take it, for
Rod was certain she never would have discarded such a
treasure.

He reached for it eagerly, then hesitated. His mother had
dosed them all with bitters, but mostly in the springtime. He
wished he had paid more attention to what she had said about
its thinning the blood. Could it harm his father? He thought
not. And it struck him that its brandy base would be the right
thing.

He took down the bottle and returned to the wounded man.
As he raised his father's inert head, the eyes fluttered open. Rod
held the bitters to the man's lips and was gratified when his
patient tried to drink. Again he offered the bitters, and this
time Mr. Wheeler took several swallows.

Rod felt of the heart. The skin around it was warming, and
the beat was stronger. He closed his eyes to pray for his father's
life. When he opened them, Will Wheeler was smiling up at
him.

Three days later, Rod took his father back to Tampa. The boy walked and let the man ride the pony, for Will Wheeler's horse had never returned to the farm. It was a slow hard trip with many stops.

Rod could have sworn his mother was crying when she saw them from the front door of the cabin, while they were still a distance away. But when they reached the house, she had the bed open, clean rags out and all her array of medicines ready.

She was brisk and businesslike as she examined the wound, which still contained the arrow head. After a keen look at her husband, she said, "Tomorrow, after you're rested, I'll take that out, Will."

She turned to Rod, laying her hand gently on his arm. "You did just right, son."

Chapter VI

Battle on the River

"On the night of the 5th, an Indian called from the
woods and hailed the camp . . . he said the Indians
were tired of fighting and desired to make peace.
The general directed an officer to tell them to come
in the morning with a white flag."

> —JOHN LEE WILLIAMS in
> *Notes from the Territory of Florida,* 1837

(Author's note: Other historians say a Negro called
across the river to Gaines' forces.)

During the month of January the Indians struck with a ferocity
peculiar to their code. Sixteen plantations in East Florida were
attacked, their occupants murdered and scalped, their buildings
burned.

There was a frantic calling for volunteers from the Southern
states. Several hundred short-term fighters from middle Florida
had already been discharged, and a new plea went out for
men who would furnish their own horses, arms and ammunition. Settlers were urged to join the militia, to aid General Call,
who now had only a hundred and fifty men in the field.

Toward the latter part of January, Major General Winfield
Scott was ordered by Washington to take charge of the war
in Florida. He would outrank General Clinch, who heretofore
had been in command. This stirred up a storm of protest from

citizens who thought General Scott an outsider, not familiar with the Territory.

Then occurred a military blunder, due to poor communications of the time, which set the countryside resounding with argument, and, according to some, prolonged the war for seven years.

Major General Gaines, on a tour of inspection in New Orleans, heard with alarm of the Dade massacre. He was told that Fort Brooke, territory within his command, was in grave danger. At once he sailed to its relief with eleven hundred recruits.

He landed at Tampa in February, found the fort intact, and at once set out with his small army to reinforce Fort King. In doing so, he ignored orders from General Scott to refrain from action.

His reasons, given later, were several and good, but the conflicting plans of the two generals were destined to hamper the operations of both.

Rod and John Fox joined the march. Rod's father was up and around again, although broad-shouldered Hughie was handling the heavy work. Hart was away, this time on a mission to the north. So the two oddly matched comrades left Fort Brooke with Major Belton and his four companies of infantry, under the command of General Gaines.

The morning was bright, the air sharp as the brigade set out along the military road in three columns. Major Belton's troops were on the right, six companies of United States infantry in the center, and a regiment of Louisiana volunteers on the left.

Rod was interested in the volunteers, who wore Army uniforms and carried Army weapons issued to them as bounty when they signed for service. They were high-spirited and eager to fight. Their lack of discipline in the ranks contrasted strongly with the trained precision of the regular troops. But they were all brave men, used to the woods, and with a hidden trace of scorn for the unquestioning obedience of Army-trained fighters. Many of them laughed and joked as they walked through the forest, and seemed to hold one volunteer's opinion that the march was not hazardous because "Lightnin' never strikes twice in the same spot."

Nevertheless, they halted in late afternoon, like the rest of the troops, and, following strict orders, erected a three-foot barrier of logs around their camp. Sentinels were posted close together, and each man was told to "sleep on his gun."

The next day, Indian signal fires were seen, and Indian riders appeared far out on the flanks of the brigade. The volunteers sobered as a brush fire flared up ahead and swept across the military road, sending red-throated clouds of smoke into the air. At night it still was burning toward the south.

It did not halt the march.

As the brigade moved northeast, and the Indian alarms increased, all signs of swagger vanished. Everyone knew they were invading Indian territory now. Would they march into an ambush? Would the Indians again try to show their strength? Many seemed to think the answer was "yes," for now there was little laughter and talk. Each man held his gun firmly, while his eyes searched the woods around.

Rod remembered something Hart Whitley had said: "To Indians, the most important thing is to surprise the enemy." If Hart was right, there would be no attack.

The brigade was still fifty miles from Fort King when rations began to run low. Although rains had slowed the march, the men had made good progress through sections of pine barren, oak hammock and the swamp areas that increased as they moved into the lake country. Some of the men began to grumble, not much caring who heard them.

"Seems like ten days' rations ain't enough," said a Louisiana farmer named Rob Walton, as he joined Rod's comrades at their campfire, "leastways to take an army into the middle of the Territory. But I s'pose the general knows what he's doing."

John Fox spoke up. "Never judge a man's brains by the gold on his uniform."

The others looked toward him, some in surprise, others ready to agree. Fox chewed on his pipe. "Provisions are plentiful at Fort Brooke, compared to Fort King. At Brooke they can be brought by schooner. At Fort King they have to be carted overland from Picolata. Figure it out for yourself."

"That's just what I think," said Walton. "We should've loaded up where there was plenty."

"Of course the brigade can stop and send out foraging parties," said Fox with gentle sarcasm. "We all know how to shoot game."

"This ain't no hunting party," growled Walton. "I got a good hound dog I could of brought if it was."

"And if we use up our powder and shot for deer, what are we going to use for Indians?" asked someone else.

That night, as he lay on the ground, trying to go to sleep, Rod was plagued, as often before, by the cynicism of John Fox. Yet he could not deny there was wisdom in the man's talk. A general wearing gold epaulettes could make a mistake, just like other men. And his mistakes would ensnare his soldiers.

General Gaines had made a mistake in moving his men without enough provisions—that seemed clear. Any attack by the Indians might have put his brigade under siege, and then they would have been in a sad condition. On the other hand, the general must know there were supplies at Fort King. Otherwise he would not have moved eleven hundred men toward that post without adequate food.

Rod thought back to the beginning of the march at Tampa Bay and of everyone's gratitude when the general arrived with reinforcements and an aggressive plan of attack. Rod himself had felt pretty noble when he joined the brigade. General Gaines must have had the same feeling.

Things certainly had changed a lot.

As sleep began to creep over him, Rod decided that hunger brought men back to earth quicker than anything else. He smiled a little as he thought that General Gaines would again be a hero if there was food at Fort King.

The next day they reached the grim spot in the trail where Rod had found the triangular fort and the dead men manning it. He turned sick at thought of seeing it again. But remembering he was in the Army, he choked back his emotion, and when orders were given he did his share in burying the company.

The fort was torn down and the men interred with military honors. Many of General Gaines' soldiers had known members of Dade's command, and some of them wept unashamedly as the funeral service moved toward a close. Others wore a stern look that suggested little mercy for the next Indians encountered.

"Fall in!"

The columns reformed.

"March!"

They moved forward.

Unfortunately, there were few provisions at Fort King. Only two days' rations could be issued to the brigade, and the men's spirits were low. Seemingly undaunted, General Gaines sent horses to Fort Drane, twenty-two miles north, and soon received food enough for eight days.

The grumble rose to a roar, which echoed faintly even in the general's ears. He ignored it. He and his men would return to Fort Brooke on Tampa Bay, he decided, but by a new route, some fifty miles west of the old one.

John Fox, who seemed to ferret out everything, informed his friends.

"But that's the heart of Indian country, ain't it?" asked

Farmer Walton. "The place they hide in and nobody can't seem to follow?"

"The very heart—the core," agreed Fox, with a sardonic flicker at the corners of his mouth. "The general is anxious to meet Indians."

"Well, so am I," exclaimed Walton, "but I'd like some good hearty eating first."

Fox laughed. Walton glared in reply. But the conversation ended there, for the brigade was ordered out almost at once and the march back to Tampa began.

Before they left, Rod was summoned by the general, who asked if his young scout knew any trails west of the military road.

"Not too well, sir," replied the boy promptly. "It's a place white men don't go. Most of the Seminoles live near the Withlacoochee cove, they say, and there are Indian villages all through there."

"Good!" General Gaines squared his shoulders under their impressive gold. "We are looking for Indians."

Rod thought of that as he walked along the trail. The columns were heading for a ford on the Withlacoochee, which the Indian guides said would do for a crossing.

The path was narrow and poorly marked. Considerable tree chopping had to be done to let the brigade through, and men cursed openly at the delay. They were disgusted, feeling they had made a long march and were having to make it again, on short rations. There was something ominous, too, about their anger—a mass presentiment of trouble.

In the late afternoon, after two days, they reached the Withlacoochee. But there was no ford at the juncture of trail and river. Men were dispatched up and down the sandy, palmetto-grown banks to find the crossing which the friendly Indians had sworn was there. No crossing could be found. There was no sign of any bridge that might ever have been used, and no shallow bars stretching into the water. The swift, deep river, almost thirty yards wide, defied the tired brigade.

Many of the soldiers broke ranks and came forward to look at the river. Rod was among them. As he stared at the opposite shore, he knew that this spot had never been a crossing. The river was too swift. Also there was a steep sand embankment on the other side that would make landing difficult, if not impossible.

As he stood there, a flick of smoke at the top of the rise caught his eye. Then came the low boom of a rifle. More wisps of smoke whipped out all along the crest of the sand wall. Gun thunder tore the quiet air. And higher pitched, bringing the same terror Rod had known at the sutler's house, sounded the long, screaming whoop of the Indians.

The soldiers scattered, seeking cover. A few staggered, wounded. Back in the woods there was a shouting of orders and men ran forward. Rifle barrels began to emerge from behind oaks, magnolias and palms.

Now the soldiers' bullets rained thick across the river, thudding against the sand embankment, kicking plumes of sand into the air. Loud yells, as ferocious as war whoops, went with every ball. A brave with red feathers stuck his head above the shelter and toppled backward at impact of a rifle bullet.

Lying flat behind a fallen log, Rod took aim with steady hand. Although it was his first battle, he was not afraid. When his bullet had sped across the river, he reloaded quickly, ramming in powder and patch-wrapped ball, priming, aiming, shooting, as if he had been under fire many times. He thought of death, but it did not frighten him. If he should be killed now, it would be an honorable death—not like being a victim of Sam Ruther's bullet.

Darkness came to end the shooting. As the sand bank grew silent, the soldiers withdrew into the woods, carrying their wounded and one dead man. In spite of casualties, the morale had tightened and courage ran high. They were fighting Indians at last.

General Gaines posted sentries and gave orders that the brigade should encamp where it was. The men were told to be ready for instant action.

The friendly Indians camped a short distance away. Word went around, from man to man, that these "guides" now said the ford was three miles down river.

At sunrise the troops were ordered downstream. After three miles of hard marching, they pushed through to the riverbank once more. Again there was no ford.

Lieutenant Izzard, popular young commander of the advance guard, rode out into the shallows, helping his men test the depth of the water. Across the stream a rifle sounded. The officer curled forward in his saddle, slid from it into the water, his blood clouding the ripples. He tried to rise, calling orders to his men.

A blistering fire opened from across the Withlacoochee, and war whoops echoed far back into the forest. Bullets feathered the surface of the river and spanged into the bank. Through their hail, three men of Izzard's command dragged their officer toward the sheltering trees. The others sprang behind thickets, fallen logs, tree trunks, whatever was handy, and sighted along their rifle barrels.

Rod had dropped behind a mass of scrub oak. He took a shot from there, then wriggled backward slowly until he found better refuge behind a wild cherry. Although it was a young growth, and slender, it was festooned with a creeper vine that offered good hiding.

Mad clear through and ready to kill, the boy aimed at a shadowy turban. Hart Whitley's counsel of reason was forgotten. Only the cruelty he had glimpsed at the sutler's, the dead men of Dade's company, and now the sight of the dying officer remained with him. The flicks of smoke across the river told him that these men were trying to destroy him. He must destroy them first.

After a time he became vaguely aware that men were felling trees in the woods back of him. He wondered why.

The fighting was still brisk when he was called away from his post. The messenger said General Gaines wanted to see him. Rod went at once to where the general stood beneath the boughs of a giant oak, looking both gallant and unsubdued.

"Rod Wheeler, sir," said Rod, saluting.

"Rod, boy," said the general, "are you acquainted with this section of the country?"

"No, sir," said Rod, "except what Hart Whitley has told me."

"What is that?"

"Just that there are a number of Indian villages near here."

"Has he never mentioned trails—or fords across the river?"

"He said there weren't any, except animal trails, or trails made by the Indians. I guess we'll have to build boats, sir, or else go back to the bridge on the military road."

"I did not ask for a plan of action, Rod."

Rod was embarrassed. "I beg your pardon, sir."

The general paced back and forth, sword swinging. "The men are cutting logs for rafts—to make the enemy think we intend to cross," he said, half to Rod, half to himself. "And I have made up my mind to build a fort back from the river. We have engaged the main army of the Indians, and I am determined to hold them until we can get reinforcements." Under his breath he added, "It may end the war."

Rod stared. This was military strategy as he had not yet learned it. His only thought had been to get the brigade across the river and back to Fort Brooke. His glance was filled with admiration for this aggressive general. His pulse beat fast with the thought that perhaps here would be the decisive battle of the conflict.

"Is there a message for me to carry, sir?"

"No," replied General Gaines. "I have already dispatched a man. Perhaps I will use you later."

Half a mile back from the water, in a broad pinewoods, the fort was begun. A loud thwacking of axes mingled with the groan of rifles along the Withlacoochee. With hundreds of men at work, the fortification went up in a hurry. It was only a breastwork, built to aid in defense of the camp, but its site was well-chosen and the stout logs made a formidable barrier.

At night the troops withdrew from the river and camped within the shelter of the new fort, well-surrounded by sentries. Fires of pitch pine were built to keep the men warm and raise their morale, for again food was low, and most of them were hungry. Rod was interested in the talk:

"We got almost the whole Indian army out there, lined up against us, I figure," said Farmer Walton. "Ain't more'n one or two thousand warriors in all, I'm told."

"That's right," agreed a regular. "If we capture them—even if we give 'em a good beating—it'll be a feather in the general's cap."

"That it would. Might make up for what he done about the rations."

John Fox sat near by, smoking his pipe and listening. He chuckled. "What strikes me funny is the fireworks this is going to cause in the Army when it's all over."

"Fireworks?" repeated Walton naively. "What fireworks?"

"Well," Fox chuckled again, "maybe you fellows don't all know that General Scott was appointed commander in chief of the Florida armies on January twenty-first. He's in charge of this part of Florida. But here we are, in the thick of it, fighting a war without orders from the top man."

The others stared at him, letting his words sink in.

"Even if we get soundly licked," Fox continued, "Scott's going to be mad. And if we round up the main body of braves and win the war—well, you say what he'll do."

Rod could hardly believe the talk. "You mean General Gaines is under General Scott's command but he's going ahead with his own campaign?" he asked.

Fox nodded. "Something like that. As I understand it, Gaines only has authority over Tampa and the western part of the Territory. He's over on General Scott's side now, running the war, and Scott's going to be mad as a black bear full of lead!"

"Golly!" exclaimed Walton as he began to see the picture.

"Funny situation, isn't it?" concluded Fox airily. "And of course if we break the strength of the Indians, General Gaines will get the glory."

"And General Scott?" asked Rod.

"A big laugh," supplied Fox.

They all chuckled, even Walton, feeling that they had the advantage of the remote General Scott. It gave them a sense of triumph that eased the tensions of the day's fight. Soon after, they all lay down to sleep, putting their faith in determined General Gaines and his sentries. They had forgotten they were hungry.

Next day the Indians made a vigorous attack. As before, the soldiers sent back volley for volley. Neither side seemed to gain or lose. The tree chopping continued, and more rafts were made.

One alarming fact came to light. Indians were crossing the river, hiding in the brush and threatening to attack or set fire to the camp.

General Gaines, who had already called for aid from General Clinch, sent another more urgent dispatch. Although Rod had been anxious to carry the message, he was not called.

Everyone grew hungrier, and the men began to talk a lot about food. General Gaines ordered that the remaining supply of corn be divided. Each man received a pint.

"What's next I wonder?" asked Rob Walton glumly, as he

sat beside the fire that evening, crunching a hoe cake he had made.

John Fox waved his pipe in the direction of the wagon horses. "Nothing left but them."

"I don't like horse meat," grunted Walton.

"Neither do I. But maybe the fight will end."

"We didn't get far today."

Fox stirred uneasily. "A lot depends on General Clinch. If he sends reinforcements . . ."

"How can he do anything else?"

"Well, so far, they haven't arrived. But we'll live, I guess," sighed Fox. "It's not the horse meat that'll kill us. Good night, fellows."

"Good night."

Fox was right about the food. Next day several horses were killed and the meat divided among the men. The following day, and the day after that, more animals were butchered. The men did not complain. They were past that. Everyone knew it was horse meat or nothing, and not one of the soldiers would have left the river while there was chance of a great victory.

Every day the Indians attacked the camp and Gaines' casualties increased. Large numbers of the enemy had crossed the Withlacoochee. They surrounded the breastwork, creeping toward it under cover of tall grass or scrub. Their yelling resounded through the woods, as if there were nothing but redmen for miles and miles.

Rod was on sentry duty the night of March fifth, standing guard on the river side of the encampment. He was hungry, as he was all the time now. As he walked back and forth at his post, between two blazed pines, he could think of nothing but the kitchen hearth at home, during Thanksgiving or Christmas holidays. He could smell and taste the turtle stew in the kettle. Sometimes it was wild turkey spitted over the coals, or a pumpkin pie just coming out of the Dutch oven.

He jerked himself back to reality. It seemed a weak thing to be so intent on his stomach. Yet a moment later his thoughts wandered back to food—Ma's cornbread this time, or blackberry pudding.

It was around ten o'clock, Rod guessed, and the moon was just showing through the thin leaf veil of the pines. A smell of pitch and the fresh odor of green things was strong here, and he was glad, for it was like being alone again on a hunting trip.

He wished he could stop walking and carve something. Since he could not, he began to practice bird calls, keeping them low and under his breath: the vireo, the meadow lark, warblers, the wild turkey. Then he imitated the yapping of the fox, the howling of a wolf and the scream of a horned owl. He became so interested that he raised his voice. As he gave the owl scream, he was startled to hear it repeated across the river.

He stopped short, shaken at the sound. It came again, but he did not answer. Then a voice cried loudly, "Soldier! Soldier!"

Instinctively Rod raised rifle to shoulder. He could not say "Halt" for the voice was across the river. Nor could he see anything at which to shoot.

The sentry posted next him ran up, shouting "Hello!"

"Soldier!" repeated the voice. It had a strangely hollow sound, as if weighted with age and weariness. "The Indians are tired of fighting and want to come in!"

Rod could hardly believe the words were spoken by a human voice. As they reverberated through the night, they seemed supernatural.

"Stay here and palaver him," said the other sentry excitedly. "I'll go tell General Gaines!"

Rod stayed, calling "Hello!" and hearing again that same statement: "The Indians are tired of fighting and want to come in!"

In a few minutes the sentry returned with Adjutant Barrow of the Louisiana volunteers. The sleepy-eyed adjutant had been sent by General Gaines, for by now the shouting had wakened half the camp.

Barrow stood behind an oak and yelled, "What do you want?" He was answered by the voice, which repeated, "The Indians want to come in and make peace!"

"Tell them to come over in the morning with a white flag," replied Barrow lustily. He repeated his words, and the strange voice answered, "I hear you. I will tell them."

By this time the whole brigade was awake and milling through the dark woods. Men gathered in clusters, whispering about the strange voice. Some thought that one of the messengers to Fort Drane had been captured by Indians and forced to yell across the river. Nearly all agreed that it was a trap of some sort.

When the new guard relieved him at his post, Rod hunted up John Fox. He found him smoking his pipe beside a dying fire.

"What do you make of it?" Rod asked breathlessly. "That voice calling—do you think it could be Indians?"

Fox shrugged. "I don't know. We'll find out in the morning —if not before."

Rod was disappointed. "I think it was the messenger," he said. "It couldn't have been Indians. They don't sound like white men."

"It could have been a Negro," said Fox carelessly.

Rod started. Why hadn't he thought of that? The Negroes spoke English as well as the whites. Many of them were fighting alongside the Seminoles, and they occupied an important spot in councils of the tribes.

"Yes," he said thoughtfully, "it could have been a Negro. I think now it was a Negro. Maybe the Indians really will come in."

"We'll know tomorrow," repeated John Fox.

Rod was too excited to sleep well. He woke at dawn and

looked toward the river for some sign of surrender. There was nothing. The rosy sunrise tinted the sandbank across the Withlacoochee, but there was no trace of Indians nor of a white flag.

The morning was silent. No rifles sounded. The sun turned warm as it climbed above the pines. Toward noon the men prepared their meal of horse meat.

Rod was spitting his meat on a long stick, when he sensed an excitement in camp. There were low-voiced whispers. Men began hurrying to the eastern end of the breastwork, crouching low and carrying their guns. But no shooting followed. Soon nearly everyone was gone from the fires, and the crowd near the logs was jostling and shoving, each person trying to look into the forest beyond without becoming a target.

Rod rose quietly, laid aside his meat and picked up his rifle. He wondered if there was any sense in joining that crowd of soldiers. As he started toward them, John Fox broke away and slapped him on the shoulder.

"It's the real thing, Rod!" he said jovially.

"What's going on?"

"The Indians have come in. Take a look."

Nearly everyone but Rod had seen, and men were laughing and shaking hands with one another. Rod pushed through the crowd and looked out across the pine barren. Through the trees and the haze of fire smoke, he could see a long line of Indians. And coming toward the fort, with a white feather in his hand was a chief in gaudy war trappings—red calico shirt, gay turban topped with plumes, necklaces of shells, face and body painted red and black. Rod caught his breath as he recognized Osceola.

On the left of the Seminole leader walked another Indian in war dress, and on his right was a very old Negro.

Adjutant Barrow came out of the fort and walked to meet the three. They came face to face in the shade of a tall pine. Osceola spoke and his message was interpreted by the Negro.

Barrow nodded and returned to the fort, sending out Captain Hitchcock to receive the word.

Rod and John Fox, watching from the fort, looked at each other triumphantly. "It's peace, Rod," said Fox. "We can tie this war up in a bundle and send it to Washington before General Scott even gets here!"

Rod was happy. Peace meant that he could go back home to his family. His father would be almost well now, and they could plant new crops—it was planting time—and the woods would be safe. It was what he wanted. And he knew that the people of Florida wanted it too.

The news that Captain Hitchcock brought was good. The Indians wished to end the fight and to have the troops leave the Withlacoochee. They would make an agreement and later bring their head chief, Micanopy, to treat with the white men.

Hitchcock conferred with General Gaines, was given instructions, and returned to the spot where he had talked to the chiefs. His orderly carried foolscap, the general's quill and ink, and the little board on which the general wrote his dispatches. Negotiations began.

General Gaines' terms, it was noised around camp, were that the Indians would return to the south side of the Withlacoochee and remain there peaceably until a formal treaty could be made with the United States commissioners. General Gaines himself had no authority to negotiate such a treaty. But he did guarantee them peace until that time.

There was considerable talking and interpreting and nodding gravely. All this the men could see from the enclosure. John Fox nudged Rod excitedly as Osceola stretched out his hand for the quill, and Captain Hitchcock pushed the foolscap toward him.

"He's going to sign!"

Rod grinned. It looked then as if the war were over. The cabin burnings, the massacres, the scalpings—all were done.

Although there still would be Indians in Florida, there would be peace, too. That seemed good enough.

But peace vanished into thin air even as they waited there for the treaty to be concluded. From among the pines, along the brigade's back trail, appeared a column of men riding on horses. At sight of the Indians, the lead riders wheeled and rode out of sight.

Fox gripped Rod's arm. "General Clinch with reinforcements! What a time to arrive! Rod, I bet you right now, the peace is done for!"

From back in the woods, rifles began to boom out their low thunder. The line of Indians burst into dozens of segments. Some warriors found refuge behind trees, fading back from trunk to trunk until they were lost in the forest. The chiefs and the old Negro turned and ran. Captain Hitchcock jumped to his feet and gestured wildly, trying to stem the firing. But the soldiers were too far away, the noise of their shooting too loud.

In a moment the woods were empty. Captain Hitchcock was in danger. His orderly had seized the inkwell and was running back to the fort. The captain followed.

Inside the enclosure, John Fox put his head in his hands. "Peace!" he moaned. "How can we hope for peace? The enemy comes bearing a white feather and we fire on them! Is there no one among General Clinch's men who can notice anything strange about this line of Indians outside the fort? Do they think we're dishing up chow?"

Rod said nothing. The belief in peace was vanishing fast, like smoke in the wind above the forest. There would be more battles, more homes destroyed, more dried scalps hanging at the waists of the warriors.

Chapter VII

Captured

"March 7 General Gaines surrendered his command to General Clinch, who with his troops retired to Fort Drane the following day."

—John T. Sprague
in *The Florida War*

In spite of Clinch's attack, the agreement with the Indians was considered a success, largely because no counterattack was made.

Two Indians and a Negro had been killed by the advance guard, but the main body of Seminoles vanished, and it was thought the chiefs planned to keep their promise. Rod learned that the "voice" was Caesar, an aged Negro who belonged to Micanopy, head of the Indians, and who, therefore, considered himself privileged among the tribes.

General Clinch had brought beef cattle to the relief of the brigade, and the hungry soldiers slaughtered several immediately and roasted themselves a meal. As the smell of cooking meat stole through the encampment, their mood relaxed to a rowdy good fellowship. Many began asking when they would be mustered out. It was only the levelheaded ones who realized that peace was not a certainty.

Next day General Gaines turned over his command to General Clinch and rode away with Captain Hitchcock. The men were held in camp another day, to their bewilderment. Their impatience was increased by a hard rain, which soaked their clothing, put out their fires and in general irked everyone. John Fox, who was always first to smell out any news, told Rod the reason for waiting.

"They've sent a Negro across the river to see what's going on. He's married to an Indian woman and the Seminoles accept him as one of themselves. He can tell us if Osceola really meant that talk about peace or if his warriors are using this time to run bullets."

Late that night the Negro returned. He reported that the Indians had taken peace seriously and had withdrawn to their villages. Their casualties were considered high—thirty warriors killed and many wounded.

"So there's still going to be peace," mused John Fox sardonically. "Well, we're lucky. But if the Indians stay in Florida, they're outguessing the U.S.A. Before this battle, we had them on the way west."

Rod knew it was true. The Indian chiefs had promised to go to Arkansas and had been given until January first to make ready. Now the rebels were trading peace for a place in the Territory. It would be a great victory for them if they were allowed to remain south of the Withlacoochee.

Next morning the troops left Camp Izzard—named after the young officer who had died there—and marched toward Fort Drane. Rod was not with them. He had asked permission to return to Fort Brooke, and General Clinch had granted it.

The rain had stopped and the river was dropping. Rod planned to go up the Withlacoochee, swim across at the first sand bar, and cut southwest. If he held to his directions, he would strike a trail that led into Tampa.

He shook hands with John Fox, Rob Walton and other acquaintances before starting upstream.

"Give the Indians a wide berth," said Fox, in warning. "This peace may not last."

Rod agreed, but forgot the words immediately as he walked along. He hoped he would be the first at Fort Brooke to bring news of the victory. He would like to tell them about the battle and the treaty.

Within seven miles, he found a bend in the watercourse where the river widened. Without too much trouble, he waded far out and swam across. Soon he was clambering up the west bank and turning south. He made no attempt to dry his clothing, but let the warm morning sunlight take care of that.

He was happily excited over going home, and the good feast on beef had made his stomach content. To walk through the woods again was a wonderful thing, after the days of hiding behind breastworks or crouching in gullies.

He couldn't help but notice the lush spring growth. Every clump of grass had multiplied by hundreds of green spears. Maidenhair fern was unrolling new fronds, and the wild grape was sending out pale tendrils with tiny leaves.

At noon he ate some cooked beef and in late afternoon he began hunting for a camping site. He found one beside a clear water hole and at once halted and looked for a place to sleep.

A Seminole campfire, shaped like the spokes of a wheel, had been made near the water, but its ashes were old and rain-soaked. Just for caution's sake, however, Rod moved far back into the underbrush. Finding a fallen log grown over with palmetto, he hollowed out a little cavern and curled up in it.

The sun was up and breaking through the thicket in small bright fragments when he woke. A throaty chuckle rang in his ears.

He started up but stopped at sight of a rifle slanting down at him. Back of the gun stood a lean, square-shouldered Indian, clad in long cotton shirt and high-wrapped moccasins. His mouth smiled grimly and his weathered face was hostile.

Next to him stood a young warrior with serious brown eyes

and a red-and-black carving around his neck. Rod did not need to look closer—the charm was a small carved bear.

"Shakochee!" he cried joyfully.

The Indian boy did not answer. He stared at Rod as if he had never seen him before.

"Don't you know me?" questioned Rod, his smile fading.

Still no answer.

"I'm Rod Wheeler!" the boy persisted, thinking Shakochee hadn't recognized him.

"Yes," said Shakochee, his face unchanging.

To Rod the word was like a blow. For a minute he couldn't talk. His eyes searched Shakochee's face but found only sternness there.

"Then what's wrong?" he asked at last, his voice strained.

Shakochee did not reply and before Rod could say more the older warrior spoke gruffly in Seminole. Shakochee obediently darted forward, picked up Rod's rifle, yanked pistol and hunting knife from the boy's belt and moved back out of reach. The square-shouldered one grunted and indicated with his gun that Rod was to rise.

Rod got to his feet, his thoughts in a painful turmoil. Why would Shakochee do this to him? Why? There seemed no comforting answer. Was it true, then, as some white folks said, that you couldn't trust an Indian? He had never believed that. Hart had said the Seminoles' ethical code was sterner than the white man's. What was wrong that Shakochee would aid in taking Rod prisoner? How could things have changed so?

Again the menacing rifle gestured—this time toward the trail.

Rod walked first, shoulders drooping despondently. The Indians followed. On the path two ponies were waiting. The man with the rifle uttered several short syllables.

Shakochee nodded agreement and cut a length of tough vine

with which he bound Rod's arms. The white boy tried to catch
his eye as he worked, but Shakochee would not look. When
the young Seminole had finished, he boosted his prisoner onto
one of the ponies and mounted in front of him. The older man
climbed onto the other pony, keeping Rod covered with his
gun. With Shakochee and Rod in the lead, they started north
along the trail.

They rode thus for several hours, moving fast, not stopping
for talk. By late morning, Rod judged they must be well up
the Withlacoochee. He groaned to himself.

They did not cross the river but continued north, along a
well-marked path parallel to the stream. All afternoon they
traveled, only stopping for water. At sundown, they came to a
trail fork, scarred by the hoofmarks of many horses. To the
left appeared a herd of ponies grazing, and farther off Rod
glimpsed cattle in a green field.

Exultant shouts arose as the riders entered the rectangular
Indian village. Rod saw open-fronted huts, where warriors
smoked their pipes, or blanketed women sewed on leather. In
the center of the clearing under a thatched shelter stood a huge
iron cook pot. Women clustered around it, stirring its contents
with a big ladle, or adding wood to the fire beneath. They
looked up at Rod, shouting, too. And the shouts were not welcoming, but exultant like those when an enemy is captured.

As the noise died down, the women turned back to their
work. Those in the cook shelter tossed more meat into the pot
and replenished the fire. Warriors resumed their smoking, but
several took up their guns.

Although Rod was scared clear through, he tried not to show
it, knowing that fear was despised among the Indians. What
would they do to him? Would he have to run a gantlet?
Would General Gaines' "peace" protect him, or was he to be a
prisoner of war?

Shakochee halted at one of the huts and dismounted, dragging Rod from his pony and pushing him toward the dwelling. The other man followed, still carrying the rifle.

Inside, the gun muzzle pointed toward a bear robe. "Sit."

Rod obeyed.

His captor spoke to Shakochee in a flood of Seminole, and the young man nodded. He went to a corner of the hut and returned with a roll of narrow rawhide, with which he bound Rod's ankles.

When the bonds were secure, the old Indian tested them, gave a grunt of approval and handed the rifle to Shakochee. Without a backward look, he left the hut and stalked across the square.

Shakochee sat, cross-legged, on the floor, beyond Rod's reach, but close enough so that Rod could see every expression of his face. He was grave now and troubled.

Rod spoke, gently. "You're no longer my friend, Shakochee. That's plain enough. What's happened?"

This time Shakochee answered, talking slowly to make his meaning clear. "Rod, you are not my enemy. You were good to me, and I cannot forget."

"Then why have you bound me like this?"

"That is because of my uncle, Tom Hadjo."

"Who is Tom Hadjo? The man who was here?"

Shakochee nodded "yes."

"Why must he have me tied up this way?"

Shakochee acted as if he did not know whether to explain further or not. At last he said, "You are his enemy."

Rod was taken aback. "That can't be," he protested. "I've never seen Tom Hadjo before. He's made a mistake."

"He has not made a mistake."

"Then what is it? What has he against me?"

Again Shakochee seemed to hesitate. "If I tell, you will not say I have told you?"

"I promise," said Rod quickly.

The brown of Shakochee's eyes seemed to deepen. "You have killed his friend," he said sadly.

Rod was too startled at first to reply. When he could speak, he opened his mouth to say he had never killed anyone. But then he remembered those battles of General Gaines' brigade, and he was silent. He did not know, for sure, that he had never killed. He had sent bullets beyond the sandbank across the river, that he knew. One of them might have killed an Indian. One of them might, indeed, have killed Tom Hadjo's friend.

At last he said in a low voice, "I have never tried to kill anyone, Shakochee, except when I was a soldier fighting an enemy. If I killed Tom Hadjo's friend, I am sorry. I am one who wants peace between the Indians and the white men."

Through the gathering shadows in the hut, Shakochee looked piercingly at Rod. "This I accept," he said. After a moment he added, "I have told Tom Hadjo about the magic you make, and about your name, Luckmaker. He knows, too, that you helped me when Sam Ruther tried to make me a slave. That is why he didn't kill you."

The words both scared and warmed Rod. "Will you free me, then?" he asked quickly. "Let me go now! Say that I tricked you."

Shakochee waited a moment to answer. "You have saved me," he said finally, "and I have saved your life for now. We are even."

Stunned at this reasoning, Rod stared at the Indian. "But I helped you get away," he reminded indignantly.

"Yes," said Shakochee, "and I am grateful. But I cannot do more."

Rod let his head sink forward. At last he knew where he stood, why he had been captured, and just why Shakochee had helped make him a prisoner. He knew, too, that his future was uncertain, dependent upon the influence of friend against enemy. And he could not fail to see that Shakochee's youth made him of minor importance where decisions were concerned. Although he had saved Rod from immediate death, he could not—as he had admitted—promise more.

Rod sat there for a long time, wondering what to say next, and at last he decided to ask, frankly, what Shakochee thought the villagers would do with him.

Shakochee did not seem surprised at the question. He gestured around the hut. "Can't you see why Tom Hadjo wants you here?"

Rod glanced at the walls and ceiling of the small dwelling. Although it was early evening, the flames from the cook fire showed him an intricate pattern of animal masks on the wall. They resembled deer, wildcat, panther and other beasts of the forest. Looped across the entrance was a row of bones, bleached dry and clean and looking oddly like medical instruments. And in the corners were strange objects which he could only half see—animal tails, teeth, strings of claws and feathers.

He was in the hut of a tribal medicine man. These were all part of Tom Hadjo's "medicine bundle," and Tom himself was a hilis-hadjo, a man versed in the dark arts of the forest, who made magic to treat and cure the misfortunes of his people.

"He wants me to carve lucky pieces?" asked Rod hesitantly.

Shakochee nodded "yes." "The one you gave me has brought luck in hunting," he said. "Tom Hadjo will ask you to make more of these, and to teach him your secrets. He will ask to know all your magic."

Rod stifled the relief that surged within him and asked warily, "What will happen when I have taught him all my magic?"

Shakochee only shrugged and looked at the floor.

Chapter VIII

Rod Makes Magic

"I don't like to make any trouble or quarrel with white people, but if they will trespass on my lands and rights, I must defend myself the best way I can, and if they do come again, they must bear the consequences. But is there no civil law to protect me? Are the Negroes belonging to me to be stolen?"

—John Walker, Indian chief,
as quoted by Capt. C. B. Marryat in
A Diary in America, 1839

The first thing Tom Hadjo did was to remove Rod's eagle charm and fasten it around his own neck. Then he asked the boy to make a carving for Gray Fox, the big chief of the village. The talisman must be a fox, painted gray.

Rod replied cautiously that he must have a fox pelt before he could carve such a charm. And when Shakochee started for the chief's home to fetch a pelt, Rod called him back, saying that his gray fox must be shot in the light of the new moon beneath a water oak.

"Why is that?" asked Tom Hadjo suspiciously in Seminole.

"It is part of the charm," said Rod.

"What if the fox is not shot as you say?" Tom pressed him.

"Then the charm will be useless."

Tom was silent. He seemed to be thinking deeply. "Let it be so," he said finally. "Shakochee, you must shoot the fox."

83

The boy nodded, but his gaze on Rod was questioning, and the white boy felt he had not fooled his friend.

In the meantime, Rod was asked to carve masks—of deer, wildcat, bear and almost every forest creature. He dared not refuse these, so he put on a secretive air and set to work, spending much time over each and astonishing himself with the excellence of his product. Tom Hadjo, too, recognized their worth, and he said so grudgingly. But back of his reluctant compliments, Rod recognized the old enmity.

Sometimes, when he wasn't busy, the white boy walked around the village with Shakochee or with Tom himself. All three could imitate bird and animal calls, and Rod's proficiency at these brought him admiration from the villagers, especially those whose skill was not as great.

He could "talk" with the woods creatures, they said.

Rod learned that the Seminoles think of animals as brothers, to be respected and treated with consideration. And from Shakochee he heard a strange folk tale of a Seminole chief who traveled through the land of the dogs and won the undying love of a beautiful lady dog before returning to his tribe to marry his Seminole sweetheart.

He heard talk of other men who spoke with the animals and perceived that the Indians both admired and feared these people. And, as he learned more of the Seminole language and the pattern of these men's thoughts, a new world opened before him.

Among themselves, the Indians dropped their air of inscrutability and became plain "village folk," who enjoyed jokes, visiting, telling stories and taking part in their own ceremonies. Although they never became friendly toward Rod, he felt their enmity decrease and hoped that if he did not escape he might some day win their liking.

Although the boy never heard talk of war, he observed that frequent councils were held by head men of the town and that little groups of young braves spoke seriously together for hours at a time. Without any attempt at concealment, they moulded bullets—far more than a hunting band could need—and toted them off each day to some secret spot.

Rod knew that when the Indians were fighting, their women made the bullets, but now, while General Gaines' "peace" seemed to hold, the women tended to their domestic tasks of smoking meat, cooking, grinding corn and fleshing hides for tanning. Later the hides would be made into garments.

Once Rod wandered over toward the Negro settlement near the village—always with Shakochee following. He saw the black men tilling fields of sprouting corn, pumpkin, squash and beans, which they would share with their Seminole masters.

Finally, when Rod had provided masks of many animals, he was asked to attempt that of a rattlesnake.

"It is Chitta-micco's magic that Tom Hadjo himself uses," Shakochee told him, as if in warning.

"Yes," said Rod, "I will make a good carving."

When the mask was completed, Rod himself couldn't help but admire the cruel look of the flat head, set with prominent poison sacs and covered with rounded scales. These last he painted with yellow made from sassafras, edging them with the black that symbolizes "death" to Indians. He held it up to show Shakochee, who had sat beside him all afternoon, his rifle across his knees.

"You did well," Shakochee assured him.

"You think Tom Hadjo will like it?"

"He will like the mask of Chitta-micco."

Dusk began to steal across the village square, and the fires cast their light into the huts and lengthened the shadows of people who approached the cook pots. Rod was surprised to see Shakochee rise, hang his powder horn and shot pouch over his shoulder and start away from the hut.

"Where are you going?" Rod called after him.

"To hunt the gray fox," replied the Indian, pointing to where a thin moon-shaving hung above the trees. "The new moon is here."

Rod had almost forgotten the new moon and the fox that he must carve. He felt a strong urge to run away, and wondered if Shakochee was leaving him alone so that he could escape. But instantly he saw that Tom Hadjo was approaching the hut.

He bent to his task of tying thongs to the Chitta-micco mask, and when Tom asked, "Where is Shakochee?" he replied glumly, "He is hunting the gray fox."

Tom said nothing, but took down his pipe and smoked it slowly. He did not look at Rod and did not see the new carving. When he finished his pipe, it was quite dark. Only the light of the cook fires danced on the walls of the hut. Rod spoke up then:

"Here is Chitta-micco."

Tom Hadjo turned sharply. As Rod held up the face of the snake, he thought how savage it looked in the flame glow. Tom Hadjo, too, must have seen the honesty of the workmanship, for Rod caught the flash of his teeth in a delighted smile before he seized the mask and held it over his face. A horrible rattling sound issued from behind the head, and a chill ran through Rod. This mask would make fine medicine indeed.

He could not repress the hope that Tom Hadjo might reward him with his freedom, but the man's next words told him what to expect.

"This is what I wanted," Tom gloated. "I will be the greatest hilis-hadjo now. There is nothing left for you to do but carve the gray fox."

Nothing left but to carve the gray fox!

The words echoed in Rod's ears. Tom Hadjo was through with him then. He had learned all of Rod's magic that he needed. Rod's weeks of safety had almost run out. When Shakochee came back with the gray fox there would be one carving left. Then would come the moment Rod feared—the hour when he was no longer of use, when he was only one of the enemy who had killed Tom Hadjo's friend.

How much time would he have? The carving could not take more than two or three days, no matter how he loitered over it. The shooting of the fox would be done tonight, for gray foxes were plentiful, and Shakochee would not dare return with empty hands.

Rod tossed and turned that night in feverish anxiety. In his dreams he saw Shakochee bring in a gray fox as big as a bear, and hand it to his uncle. The white boy woke in a sweat, resolved to stay awake till dawn, but drifted again into tortured sleep.

The sky was faintly rose-colored when the young Indian returned. Rod heard him come into the hut, heard Tom Hadjo rouse and say, "Have you brought the fox?"

"There are no gray foxes tonight," replied Shakochee briefly. "I have hunted the night through and the new moon is gone."

"But I have promised the chief!" protested Tom angrily.

"Then I will try again next month." The boy's words were blunt and final, as if he expected punishment for them.

For a long time Tom Hadjo was silent. Then he remarked, "Next time I will hunt, too."

Nothing else was said. Shakochee lay down to sleep, while Tom and Rod got up and went to the cook pot in the square, for soon the sun would burst over the horizon and all the villagers would be at their daily tasks.

Rod did not speak, repressing the joy that was in him. For Shakochee had saved him again—that he knew. He had gained a month's reprieve. He was positive now that he had a friend.

Two weeks raced past, without offering Rod a chance of escape. His thoughts now were fixed on running away. He weighed this scheme and that, searching frantically for one that might be successful. Although there were times when he might have eluded Shakochee and have darted into the woods around the camp, he dared not try. The many braves would have given instant pursuit. Even if Shakochee failed to send a bullet after him, there were dozens of others who would.

He watched for a chance to steal the Indian boy's gun—or Tom Hadjo's. But no such time ever came.

At night Tom Hadjo brought in three large dogs and taught them to sleep across the front of the hut. Now there was less opportunity than ever to fade into the woods under cover of darkness.

Rod thought of making friends with the dogs and walking past them some night. But progress was slow, for they were surly, and he knew one growl would warn the sentries who sat all night beside the fire in the square, or perched in the tall lookout tree over the river.

To make things worse, Rod heard rumors of new white armies preparing to march from both East and West Coasts. And beneath their outward quiet, the Indians seemed to grow tense. If war came again, there would be no such thing as safety among these people.

Escape he must. But how? Rod could see no way.

He looked often at the ponies in the grassy pasture and tried to figure out which horse he would take if he had a chance. He speculated, too, about the dugout canoes which lined the riverbank and wondered if it would be easier to paddle down river in one of them than to run or ride out of camp.

Without any definite plan in mind, he looked at the herbs hanging in Tom Hadjo's corner of the hut, and the idea came that perhaps Tom's medicine bundle contained the answer. It might include something that would put the dogs to sleep or even Tom Hadjo himself.

Rod questioned Tom in an offhand manner, to see if he would talk about the bundle. But the man only met his remarks with an inscrutable stare.

"I have medicines," ventured Rod in his halting Seminole, "about which I have not told you."

"What have you?" asked Tom, interested.

Rod hesitated a moment, then plunged. "Tell me first what your medicine bundle contains."

Tom Hadjo looked at him piercingly, as if he suspected a trick. At last he said, "You would make a great hilis-hadjo, were you one of us. But you are an enemy. And besides, my bundle is secret. I can tell what is in it only to Shakochee. He has worked for many summers so that he can have a medicine bundle of his own."

Rod said no more. He had failed again. It seemed as if there was no way out. The month would pass and the gray fox would be caught. Or war would come and again he would be an active enemy. He could not think what to do.

He began urging Shakochee to go with him to the riverbank, under pretext of hunting for a certain blue stone, which was said to be lucky. The stone was a product of Rod's imagination, but it brought them to the bank of the Withlacoochee River and kept them there, searching up and down the banks.

Rod made careful note of the canoes which the braves used to go up and down the river. Most of them were small, but there was one larger dugout, very old and somewhat lop-sided, that stayed at its mooring all the time.

He pointed it out to Shakochee. "That strange canoe—that does not sit straight. Who could paddle in that without falling into the water?"

Shakochee looked up from his search for the blue stone. "That is a good boat," he said gravely. "It is old, but it goes fast."

"Then why doesn't anyone use it?" asked Rod.

"It belongs to the lookout in the tree."

Rod glanced up into the giant oak that towered over the river just above the old cypress canoe. Yes, there was the lookout, sitting quietly in the crotch of a limb high above ground. His rifle rested on a branch in front of him and his eyes were fixed far off, as if he watched for something or someone that would come soon.

He was a long way from his canoe, Rod observed cannily. If ever there was a chance to cut that boat loose and whirl down river, he would take it.

But he waited vainly. Shakochee stuck as close as a burr; even Tom Hadjo was around the hut most of the day. Rod gathered from stray bits of talk that Indian scouts had been sent to discover if a new white army would invade their territory.

The time of grace grew shorter and Rod's hopes dwindled each day. His constant small failures took a big toll of his optimism, and without realizing it he sank into a state of discouragement. He began to believe he would never get away. His hopes turned toward the possibility that he might be traded to white armies in return for a Seminole prisoner, but the chance was remote, and he knew it. In his spare time he began to carve a message on a rock, just in case he never reached home again.

Rod Wheeler
taken by Indians
March 1836

Chapter IX

Shakochee Pays His Debt

"The black drink is used by the head-men of the Seminole nation, preparatory to the assembling of important councils. It is drunk three times a day, for seven consecutive days. This process, it is thought, cleanses the system, and gives to the mind wisdom and clearness."

—JOHN T. SPRAGUE
in *The Florida War*

In Shakochee's heart there was a profound sorrow for this friend of his. He had watched Rod search for the rock on which he was carving his message, and now he stared as the white boy chipped out the words.

The morning was warm, with the sun dappling the inside of Tom Hadjo's hut. In the forest, clouds of tender green bloomed on the oaks, and every day Shakochee saw new birds flying north. He had pointed them out to Rod, but the boy did not answer, and Shakochee knew he had lost hope.

Even Shakochee himself was worried. For he could not delay catching the gray fox again. Tom Hadjo was sure to send someone with him this time, and the animal must be brought in. Then would come the end of Rod's magic.

Idly Shakochee noticed a bustle of preparation around the cook pot. Several women, talking excitedly, threw fresh meat into the kettle, and others brought wood to stoke the fires.

91

Something was going on, the Indian boy decided. He would have to find out what it was.

Soon the commotion centered at the far end of the village. Shakochee stiffened as he saw horses coming into the square. He noted two warriors, both strangers to him. His eyes widened abruptly as they lighted on a white man riding a bright roan. Behind the roan came a tall Negro astride an Indian pony.

A rising anger simmered within Shakochee as he watched the group turn toward the hut of the chief. What was Sam Ruther doing here? And why was he accompanied by warriors? Surely he was a captive—and yet the pomp and ceremony attending his entrance suggested that he was an honored visitor.

Shakochee watched closely as Ruther dismounted and went into the chief's hut. As the villagers began drifting in that direction, he called to a young brave.

"Soleta!"

At the call, Rod looked up. It was the first time he had gazed into the square for a good half hour. He glanced toward the crowd of Indians with an air of disinterest and returned to his work.

Soleta paused and Shakochee urged quickly, "Stay here for me and guard the white boy! I will tell you what goes on."

Soleta shook his head. "Someone has come into camp. I want to find out who it is."

"Stay here," insisted Shakochee sharply. And, as the Indian turned to leave, "I will give you my shell bracelet."

Soleta hesitated. His curiosity was strong, but the shell bracelet was a prized possession.

"I will stay," he said.

He stepped inside the cabin, took Shakochee's rifle and glared fiercely at Rod, as if to make his prisoner afraid. Shakochee, without a word, jumped to the ground and hurried away. He did not speak to Rod, for he knew the boy would soon see the visitors and recognize them. Besides, a blazing anger choked the young Seminole and kept him silent.

With the light grace of an animal, he ran—not to the chief's house but to the home of Catsha, near by. Catsha was a powerful member of the council and of greater influence than Tom Hadjo. He could speak fluently and often swayed the villagers to his way of thinking. Sometimes he put words into the mouth of the old chief himself.

He sat now on a bear rug in the open door of his hut, smoking slowly, his broad face deeply marked with squint wrinkles. His scalp lock held a buzzard feather, to show that he could doctor gunshot wounds.

He glanced at the boy who stood outside. "Come," he invited without smiling.

Shakochee stepped into the hut. Now that he was here, he did not know what he could say. There seemed no way to get that burning anger outside of his body, no words to tell how he felt.

"I have just seen a white man," he faltered, halting as Catsha's eyebrows rose a trifle.

"Yes, Shakochee."

The Indian boy struggled to speak, and the words came abruptly, "He is a man of evil!"

Catsha did not blink. He nodded and smoked his pipe, without any sign of surprise. At last he spoke. "The man named Ruther is here. He has come to trade."

"He is a man of evil!" repeated Shakochee excitedly. "Catsha, he is the one who struck me on the head and tied me. He would have made me a slave! Did you not know?"

Catsha released a cloud of smoke and said gently, "He is the same."

"But Catsha . . ." protested Shakochee.

"I am sorry," the older man interrupted, "but we must have

him here. It is worse than that. We must even pretend to honor him."

"Honor him!" Shakochee's world seemed to spin around. He could not believe he had heard the words. "Did you say honor?" he stammered.

Catsha nodded, waggling the buzzard feather. "We must honor him now," he said. "Perhaps some day we can treat him as we think he should be treated, for I, like you, Shakochee, know he is a man of evil. He has enslaved our Negroes, and those of other Indians. And it is said he has captured Indians, too, and shipped them to northern plantations."

"Then why . . . ?"

Catsha held up his hand for silence. "He has something our village needs. Have you not heard, Shakochee, that white armies wait to march from the east? The war is on again. There will be no peace, as the white men said. There is a new general now—one named Scott. He makes war," Catsha checked Shakochee's question with a gesture and added, "and for war we must have powder and guns. These we can trade for with Ruther. This we must do."

Shakochee was silent. He had heard the rumors. He had hoped they were not true. And he knew, too, that many of the guns in the village were old, and that some warriors had lost theirs because they hunted in white-man territory.

"Could we not take the guns and powder from Sam Ruther and imprison him?" he asked at last. "Then he could be tried before the council—and I could tell what I know."

"These are things for the council to decide," the older man rebuked him.

Shakochee turned away. He could not bear to have this hated Ruther inside the Indian village, nor to know that the chief was treating him courteously. It violated the boy's sense of honor and hurt even worse than had his great blaze of anger.

Now the anger had turned into a lump of grief, and Shakochee was afraid the tears would come, to his everlasting shame.

He walked rapidly, angling off into the forest at the first path. His thoughts were tumbling into ruin. All his life he had been taught that honor came first—before food or pleasure or safety. Now it seemed as if honor were lost to him and the people of his town through their dealings with Ruther.

Sometimes he ran, when the grief pressed hardest. Again he walked, pausing cautiously, out of sheer habit, when a squirrel scolded or a bird gave its alarm cry, until he saw that the trail was clear.

When darkness began to seep into the woods, he turned back toward camp. His sorrow had sunk deep within him, and he knew it would no longer show in his face. But it would remain, secret and hidden, a scar on his belief in the Indian code.

He would never speak of what had happened, he decided. Some day, perhaps, when he was a medicine man and a power in the village, he would hold firm against such as Ruther. The old code—a life for a life—would be upheld. Then such a man would become a slave.

For perhaps half an hour after Shakochee had left the hut, Rod sat quietly, his thoughts going back to the hopelessness of escaping. At first he had eyed the new guard with interest, but the fellow's ugly look and his significant shaking of the rifle now and then told Rod what to expect.

He wondered idly why Shakochee had gone, but it was not for some minutes that he noticed the two strange horses which stood in front of the chief's dwelling.

Instantly he recognized the bright roan. Although he neither moved nor spoke, the skin of his back seemed to curl and prickle, as if a warning finger had touched him. There could be no doubt the horse was Sam Ruther's—there was no animal so red or deep-chested in the whole western territory. The little pony, while not distinguished by any special markings, confirmed Rod's identification of the other horse.

"Who talks with the chief?" he asked Soleta.

Soleta only glared and shook his rifle.

"Is it Sam Ruther?" Rod persisted.

But Soleta would not answer.

Another half hour passed and Rod saw two warriors go into the chief's hut. They came outside in a moment and walked briskly toward the house of Tom Hadjo.

Rod sensed approaching disaster. He was not surprised when the men halted before him. The taller of the two said to Soleta, "The chief wishes Luckmaker to come to his house."

Soleta only stared.

"Put your gun away," the man said sternly. "We have come to take Luckmaker."

Slowly Soleta set his gun against the wall of the hut. The warrior gestured to Rod. "Stand."

Rod got to his feet. There was no use resisting. Nor would he act afraid.

"Go," ordered the brave, training his gun on Rod's ribs. "Go to the house of the chief."

Although his head was spinning with confused thoughts, Rod held it high and did as he was told. At the chief's hut he was ordered to halt.

Ruther and the wrinkled old warrior were sitting on the floor, smoking together; now they paused to look at Rod. Ruther's eyes were cold, but in their yellowish depths Rod thought he saw a deep pleasure. The boy stared back boldly although his heart was pounding.

With slow reluctance the slaver spoke. "Yes, I will trade. He's the son of a farmer I know. What do you ask?"

The chief chewed his pipe, considering. His faded eyes appraised Rod as if the boy were a pony he wished to trade. "Ten kegs of powder," he said finally.

Ten kegs of powder! Rod could not believe that the Indians held him so cheap. Yet his tumbling thoughts told him that ten kegs of powder would kill many white men.

"Too much," growled Ruther. "He is not a good friend."

There was a long silence. Finally the slaver added, "I will give five. And that's a high price."

"Ten kegs of powder," repeated the chief.

Ruther shifted uncomfortably. "He's not worth that to me," he grumbled. "Two kegs would be my price, except that I know the lad."

He waited for an answer, but none came. At last he said, "Will you take five kegs?"

"I have said ten kegs," replied the chief firmly. "He is Luckmaker. He works for us in good ways. I would not trade him for less than ten kegs."

Ruther's eyes passed scornfully over Rod, as if he were thinking, "Ten kegs of powder just for this insolent fellow!" But he said aloud to the chief, "Ten then. Send your warriors for them."

"Good." The chief puffed slowly on his pipe. "Take the boy."

"Dan'l!" called Ruther sharply. And when the big slave ambled forward, "Tie this Luckmaker. We'll take him with us tomorrow."

Rod pressed his lips tightly together as Big Dan'l began to bind his arms. Panic swept over him, but he did not cry out. When the rawhide thongs were tight around his wrists, Dan'l bound his ankles.

"Take him to the wagon," ordered Ruther.

Dan'l picked Rod up as if he were a bundle of hides and slung him easily over his shoulder. Then with long strides he carried the boy back of the chief's hut to the edge of the woods. A wagon stood there, its horse unhitched and cropping grass near by. Two Indians were unloading powder and rifles. Big

Dan'l waited until the wagon was empty, then dumped Rod into it. Relieved of his burden, the slave climbed onto the driver's seat and sat there, silently watching the woods and the activity of the villagers.

Rod's bruised cheek lay against the bottom of the wagon in a heap of spilled gunpowder. The stuff burned his skin and nostrils, but he hardly noticed. One thought absorbed him. He must get away now, or he would never again be free. Ruther had tried to kill him once. No telling what he would do this time.

Rod turned his head and glanced cautiously at Big Dan'l, remembering that the black man had worn his eagle charm. Did that thong around his neck still hold the luck emblem?

"Dan'l," he called.

Dan'l turned and stared at the boy on the wagon floor.

"Do you wear the charm I carved?"

In answer, Dan'l pulled the eagle from beneath his shirt.

"Has it brought you luck?"

"Good luck," replied Dan'l, nodding vigorously. "No bullet hit me I wear this."

"My charms are good," said Rod, his confidence increasing. "Let me make you another."

He waited a full minute, but Dan'l did not answer, nor display any interest. Apparently one charm was enough.

"Look, Dan'l," Rod urged, "I could carve you a lucky piece in the shape of a gray fox. The hilis-hadjo here would trade anything for it."

Still Dan'l showed no interest.

Rod racked his brain for the thing that would appeal to Dan'l, but could turn up nothing. Big Dan'l himself gave the clue. "You carve lucky piece against whip?" he asked abruptly.

Whippings! Of course. Rod had almost forgotten that Ruther beat his big slave into submission. He thought fast.

"I could carve you a rattlesnake," he offered. "The Indians call her Chitta-micco—ruler of the beasts. She has a sting worse than the whip."

Dan'l looked at him, a gleam of hope in his black face. "She would scare the whip?"

"The whip would not dare bite you if you wore Chitta-micco," said Rod, hoping he would be forgiven for telling this lie to save his life.

The Negro's eyes flamed with eagerness. The curls on his head quivered. "Make me a Chitta-micco," he urged roughly.

Rod held up his bound wrists. "Cut me loose, then, and lend me your knife."

The big man reached for his knife, but his hand did not draw it from its sheath. The excitement faded from his face and his eyes grew crafty.

"I need my hands to carve a charm," Rod reminded him quietly. "I cannot make Chitta-micco if I am tied."

The hand drew the knife part way out of its sheath, then rammed it back again. "No," said Dan'l, his voice flat.

"Why not?" pressed Rod.

The big slave's face was blank. "No," he said again.

Rod held up his wrists. "It will take only half an hour," he urged. "No one will see."

But Dan'l struck Rod's arms downward angrily, and the boy dared not say more. He lay quietly in the bottom of the wagon, his spirits dropping down and down. Big Dan'l could not be fooled. And there was no chance of wriggling free, for his tight bonds were already biting into his flesh and his ankles were swollen.

As night crept across the village and the stars began to glimmer in the sky above, Rod wondered vaguely if he would be given food or water. But apparently no one planned such kindness. Dan'l ate a handful of corn from the depths of his pocket and said nothing to Rod about supper.

A little later, when the woods were black and only the light of a half moon outlined the big man, Rod saw that his guard was asleep. For a few minutes the boy's hope revived. But it faded as he tugged vainly at his bonds, feeling his utter helplessness.

He wondered what his father would do in such a spot, and at once he knew. Will Wheeler believed in the power of prayer. He would have prayed instead of thinking up lies to save himself. So Rod closed his eyes and whispered, "Please help me, Lord."

The words quieted him, and his panic lifted. At least now he could be brave, no matter what happened. Now he could face Ruther and take the worst he had to offer.

Somewhere in the dark hours, well past midnight, Rod dozed. He was wakened by a whisper so soft that it might have been the wind.

"Luckmaker!"

He opened his eyes, wondering if he had dreamed that word.

It came again. "Luckmaker!"

Rod stirred. At once he felt a hard pressure against the thongs on his ankles. There was a slight creak of knife against leather, then miraculously his legs were free.

"Come."

He did not wait for urging. Moving slowly, so he would not rouse the sleeping Dan'l, Rod sat up, got to his knees, then to his feet. Shakochee's hands reached over the wagon side to help him out. In another second the two boys were hurrying into the black woods.

At first Rod's feet felt dead and nerveless, but as he ran the blood flowed back into them and they carried him swiftly. When he and Shakochee were half a mile into the forest, the Indian halted. He drew out his knife and cut the hide around Rod's wrists.

"Go now," he said. "Run for the rest of the night and hide in the morning. White armies are coming, and we are moving from the village. You will see our people on the trails tomorrow. Hide well, for I cannot help you again."

He thrust the handle of the knife into Rod's palm and ran back toward the square.

Gripping the weapon, Rod sped in the other direction. A sense of haste and a wild feeling of victory were jumbled together inside him, along with a tender gratitude to the Indian boy. Shakochee's goodness, he vowed, he would never forget. Not to the last day of his life. For Shakochee now had saved him twice—once from the vengeance of Tom Hadjo and again from Ruther.

Through the woods he raced, stumbling over bushes and vines, but following old deer trails as best he could in the dimness of the moonlight. At last he struck the broad main trail to the south and the going was easier. Still he dared not stop, except to catch his breath. When he could run again, he plunged onward, knowing he must leave the village behind him.

As the sky brightened in the east, he began to look for a hiding spot. Shakochee had said to hide, and besides Rod was breathing hard, for the long imprisonment had cost him both wind and strength.

At first he could not find a place. There were fallen trees, their lifeless branches looped with moss, but nothing that satisfied him. One sapling was draped so thickly that the moss made a little tent, but Rod passed it by, thinking it drew attention to itself by its odd shape.

The birds began to flutter through the tops of the trees, and the sun's rays touched the crest of the forest. Still Rod had not found a shelter. He was beginning to worry, for some warrior might be ahead of the others, following this trail, and the boy knew he must leave it.

The scolding of a squirrel drew his attention. There it was, peeking out of a hole high in an oak. Rod's pulse pounded. A hollow tree!

He moved toward it, pleased at the thick growth of palmetto around its base. When he parted the fans, a cavernous hole met his eyes. Moving carefully so as not to crush or bend any bit of undergrowth, he crept into the tree and drew the fans across the hole. Above him, the squirrel began to fuss. Rod threw a bit of rotting wood at him and he darted away.

The hollow was small. Rod could barely get inside and draw his knees close to his body. A faint animal odor came from the spot, and Rod could feel silky bits of fur mixed with rotting wood on the ground. Wisps of cobweb caught on his head, and he slapped at a spider that bit him. He hoped fervently that it was not the poisonous black one with the red hourglass on its belly.

Outside the wood was still, and, tired from his long run, he slept.

He was roused by the distant sound of a horse's whinny. At once he was wide awake, listening. From the direction of the trail came faint noises, the tramping of many hoofs.

Taking care not to ruffle the tops of the palmettos as he moved, Rod wriggled out of the tree, feet first. His legs were numb from being cramped close to his body. Once in the open, he turned over, slowly, and raised head and shoulders above the palmetto fans.

The forest was a tender, luminous green beneath the noonday sun. From where he lay he could see nothing but trees, vines and moss. But the sounds were clearer here. The thud of hoofs on the soft ground came to him plainly.

Were the Indians heading south? He must know. Moving slowly toward the trail, he wormed his way into a dense thicket near its edge. From there he could see the path to the south.

Shakochee had told him the truth. The villagers were on the move. They had loaded their ponies with all their possessions —hides, kettles, haunches of smoked venison, sacks of corn and coonti, lead, gunpowder and whatever they must carry with them. Even the cypress canoes were tied onto the ponies' backs.

He did not see Tom Hadjo nor Shakochee. At the end of an hour, the cortege suddenly dwindled to nothing. Two or three Indian braves, riding without packs, marked the end of the procession. They had been put there as a sort of rearguard, Rod thought.

When they were gone, he crept back to his tree, slid inside its warm darkness and went back to sleep, remembering what Shakochee had said about hiding all this day.

After a long time of broken slumber, he roused. His legs were dead again, and his stomach hurt with hunger. There was no light at the tree entrance so he moved outside.

It was night, and the clean smell of the air, the sight of a star shining down through the oak branches was infinitely good after the stuffiness of the tree. He took long breaths of air as he stood up and stretched himself.

The moonlight, broken into pale bits by the tree branches, hung on the undergrowth like luminous flowers. Night sounds were loud around him.

He was used to being hungry and was quite willing to start a night's walk without food, but his thoughts turned involuntarily to the good sofke he had eaten in the Seminole village. And as he remembered the smoked meats hanging from the cookhouse rafters, he had an exciting idea.

Why not go back there and gather up the scraps the Indians had left? In their haste, they must have forgotten something. He could gather provisions for the long trip south, wait until the villagers were well ahead of him, and then begin his journey.

As he started north along the main trail, he became even more optimistic. Perhaps someone had left a gun and some powder! Deep down, he knew this was a foolish hope, but it helped him to stride fast along the trail.

Soon he heard the rumble of the Withlacoochee River and knew he was approaching the deserted town. Then came the broad place in the path where the cattle were driven to their pasture, and then the square.

At the end of the camp he paused, staring at the rows of dark huts and the white ashes under the cook shelter. A faint sound drew his attention to the lookout tree. His gaze, flicking up along the moon-brightened toe holds, stopped at a dark shadow near the top. The sentry! He had stayed here to watch for the enemy's coming and bring word of it.

Rod drew back, his good mood ebbing. Here, indeed, was trouble. But even as his hopes fell, a strange excitement surged through him. The old canoe! If the lookout were still here, so was the canoe!

Heart on fire, he moved softly back on the trail and made a wide circle of the abandoned settlement, coming toward it from the west. Now he was much closer to the lookout tree and the curve of the river. Keeping within cover of the shadows, he peered along the bank of the stream, to see if the canoe really was there.

By leaning far out and taking a step into the current, he could glimpse one end of a dugout, pulling gently against its mooring as the river sucked at it. He leaned out again, his hopes soaring. Yes, it was the old canoe! The lopsided one that went fast!

He felt like shouting. But he only drew his foot out of the water and crouched on the bank, wondering how he could reach his boat without being seen, for by now it seemed as if the old dugout belonged to him alone.

In the back of his mind, he knew he must work fast. The lone sentry might climb down his tree at any moment, step into the canoe and paddle hastily away, beyond reach of white armies.

Rod gritted his teeth, determined to get the canoe first. If he could cut it loose, without being seen, he could lie in the bottom of the craft and let the current pull him downstream.

Across the river, chuck-will's-widows were calling. They would furnish a cover of sound. Night shadows would hide him. If he was careful, he could make it.

Moving with painful slowness and only when the birds called, he took step after step along the bank toward the canoe. At each yard gained, his spirits rose. At last he had just a short fifteen feet to go. But it was a crucial distance, for the lookout tree was now only some sixty feet away.

The growth here was pine and water oak, with a tangled ground carpet of saplings and dwarf palmetto. As he stepped into it, he heard an alarmed twittering. He halted. The twittering spread through the trees. There was a sudden flutter, a squawking, and then the screaming jabber of a flock of parakeets as they rose into the air.

The betraying beat of their wings struck through Rod. Without time to think or plan he crashed ahead, gained the canoe. With a hard slash of his knife, he freed it from its mooring. One tremendous shove sent it skimming out into the river. As it left the shallows, Rod leaped into it and dropped flat.

Above him the parakeets circled out over the water and back toward the bank, still crying. Through their din he heard the sentry's challenging shout in Seminole. On impulse he shouted back, in Shakochee's tongue: "Don't shoot! Don't shoot!"

The cry probably saved his life. The sentry hesitated as the canoe moved to the center of the river. There the current caught it like a floating twig, straightened it out and sent it whirling downstream.

The rifle roared and a bullet plumped into the water. That was the last. Before the sentry could reload, Rod was out of gun range, hidden by the massive tree growth along the banks of the dark river.

Chapter X

In the Blockhouse

"Troops in the late campaign suffered severely from
sickness—more than one-half were at different times
disabled by sickness, most of which was the measles."

—A Lieutenant of the Left Wing
in *Sketch of Seminole War,* 1836

Rod's hands trembled as he felt in the bottom of the canoe for
an oar. There was nothing but a crude pole—a pine branch
with sap oozing out of it and rough spots where the smaller
branches had been lopped off.

He sat up carefully, lowered the pole over the side and tried
to touch bottom. It was a foolish move—the current snatched
at the pole and his dugout swayed violently. He drew back his
"oar," deciding it could be used only as a rudder.

It didn't matter. The river was fast. He could guide himself
around stones or fallen trees, and soon he would be far away
from the Indian village. When he wanted to land, he could
watch for a fallen tree or steer himself into some back eddy.

Although the dugout was of fair size and swift, it was sensi-
tive to every shift of weight. As soon as Rod raised himself
a little too high, it rocked perilously.

The swift movement of objects and water made him slightly
dizzy, so he looked up at the stars and was steadied. Carefully
he gauged his position and figured out the time.

A deep satisfaction bubbled up in him. Although he was still on the Withlacoochee and deep in Indian territory, he had escaped Ruther and was once more headed for home. He was hungry, but tomorrow he could land and trap a bird or animal. His route was roundabout, but he wasn't lost. He even had hopes of reaching the Gulf and signaling a schooner which would take him into Tampa Bay.

Ahead, something loomed in the river—a tree, fallen from the bank and lodged against an island in the center of the stream. Rod grabbed the pine pole, dropped it out the back of the dugout and pressed hard against the water. The craft veered sharply right, skimmed around the log and slowly moved back to the center current.

Perturbed by his narrow escape, Rod sat for hours with the pole in his hands. With the moon high, he could see a good distance along the glistening dark path of the river. He wished the moon weren't so bright. He would make a good target from shore. But there was nothing to do about it except keep low in the dugout. He was afloat, and until he was ready to land, it would be better to take his chances here.

The motion of the water made him drowsy and the soft rumble of its current was a throaty night song. Toward morning the desire to sleep became irresistible.

Dared he try it? He answered himself with an emphatic "no!" It was important to see obstacles and steer around them. Yet in spite of his resolve, his head dropped forward and he dozed. Sharply he wakened, saw that everything was all right and dozed again. Sleep stole more deeply into him, and without knowing it he lay down in the bottom of the boat, head pillowed on one arm.

The roar of a rapids tore through him. He sat up, scared. The sky was softly red, like a flamingo feather. The rising sun was still just a brightness above the tips of the trees. Ahead the dark river widened, and its surface was gashed with rock from shore to shore. Around the rocks, water flowed whitely, making the noise he had heard.

He seized his pine stick and thrust it into the current. But there was no safe water ahead. Frantically he turned his craft toward shore. It was too late. The cypress canoe, gliding lightly downstream, struck a rock, shuddered violently and swung away. Swiftly it whirled around, glanced sidewise against another rock and hit prow on against a third.

Rod never knew when the boat upset. He only felt the cold chill of the water closing over him and the pummeling hands of the current that hurled him against rocks, brought him to the surface and pulled him down again. Now and then he glimpsed the rosy sunrise, but mostly he was careening through a half-dark world of bubbles and tugging water.

He was bruised and half drowned when at last his feet struck bottom. The current had relaxed, and he was able to stand. He was below the rapids, in a backwash. Instinct helped him to stagger ashore, where he lay on his stomach, coughing and retching, getting up the water he had swallowed.

After a while he could breathe. The warmth came back into his body. He knew he would be all right.

He raised his head and looked around him. He was at the western end of a dense hammock. The interlacing arms of the oaks were laden with moss and air plants; willows grew thickly along the water, and near by the huge white blossoms of a magnolia reflected the red of the sunrise.

He looked for his boat. It was nowhere in sight.

Remembering that he must hide in case there were Indians here, he got up, crept into the shelter of the woods and lay down beneath a broad-fanned palmetto. His body hurt in a dozen places. He touched them with his fingers, to see if any bones were broken, or if the flesh was torn. His bones seemed whole, and there was only a shallow cut in the calf of one leg.

I'm lucky, he thought and realized that he was without his carved eagle.

Still tired and breathing hard, he lay there and rested, wondering how far it was to the Gulf. He had heard of a rapids some ten or fifteen miles from the mouth of the river. Maybe he could walk the rest of the distance.

Slowly the silvery chop-chop-chop of an ax worked its way into his consciousness. He stiffened in alarm.

Ears alert, he waited, hoping to figure out how far away the sound was. If Indians were cutting logs for some of their huge, wheellike campfires, he must be very close to their village.

The ringing noise of the ax continued. Soon another joined it, then another until the forest was filled with the blow of axes against pinewood.

Rod raised his head. Where had he heard that sound before —or one exactly like it? Then it came to him. This ping of axes was exactly like that of General Gaines' army building its fortification on the Withlacoochee!

He stood up quietly and moved through the woods in the direction of the chopping. As the sound of axes grew louder, he heard a humming beneath it. The hum rose and fell. Men talking!

His heart beat loudly as he crept closer. At last, through the trees, he could see them.

Ten or twelve soldiers in the fatigue uniforms of the United States Army were cutting pines at the edge of a small clearing. Others were lopping branches or trimming the logs to a point at one end. A team of four men was snaking the logs toward a fortification they were building around a small blockhouse.

All were talking seriously, some smoking as they worked, one or two chewing tobacco or snuff.

"Hallo!" shouted Rod.

The result was startling. The men dropped their axes and their logs. Each grabbed up his gun and ran scrambling to the blockhouse. The door was too small for them all to enter at once, and there was a pushing and shoving to get in. One stumbled and was knocked flat. But when the others had jumped over him, he got up and ran inside, too. The door was slammed shut and Rod saw rifle barrels pop out from the loopholes of the little fort.

He would have laughed if it hadn't been a life or death matter. If one of those men sighted him, he was as good as dead. The whole garrison was ready to turn their guns on him, and he would be riddled with bullets.

He had to do something in a hurry, so he shouted: "I'm a white boy! My name's Rod Wheeler!"

He shouted this several times before he saw some of the rifles withdrawn from the holes.

"I've been with General Gaines' brigade," he added. "Let me come in!"

This, too, had to be repeated. At length the door of the fort was opened, and someone answered, "Come on in!"

Rod hated to walk out of the shielding hammock into the muzzles of those suspicious rifles. But there was no choice. He cried out, "All right. Here I come."

Holding his hands high above his head, he walked into the clearing. One step, two, three. No shots. He kept going. If only some idiot doesn't shoot anyway, he kept thinking.

At the halfway mark he was still alive. Someone inside the fort began to laugh. Others took it up. The gun muzzles were withdrawn. Then, gradually, the men began to drift out the door. They were smiling and shamefaced. They came toward Rod, their commander at their head.

"Rod Wheeler, sir," said Rod, clicking his heels together and saluting as he came up to the sun-browned young man, who wore the insignia of a captain. "I've served at Fort Brooke, sir, as express and guide. I went out with General Gaines and was with him on the Withlacoochee. When I tried to get back to

Fort Brooke I was captured by Indians and I've just made my way here, sir."

"I'm Captain Halliman, Rod," said the officer, "in command here until our Major McLemore returns. Come inside, boy, I want to talk with you."

Rod followed the captain inside the blockhouse. It was dark and he could just see that several men were lying around the walls on pallets. At sight of Rod, one of them rose up on an elbow and saluted.

"Rod Wheeler! Well, I never!"

Rod stared. The voice was Hart Whitley's. His eyes strained through the dimness, unbelieving. Although the bearded man on the floor looked curiously puffy around the eyes, Rod saw that he had the same thoughtful forehead and determined jaw of his old friend.

"Hart!" he exclaimed. And then, cloaking his surprise, "Reporting for duty, sir."

Hart chuckled. "Rod is my protégé, Captain Halliman. He's as smart in the woods as an Indian—and Major Belton trusts him farther." And as Rod reached out a hand, "Wait, fellow! Don't touch me! Can't you see something funny about me? Stand back!"

"What is it?" asked Rod, puzzled. "You do look different. What's the matter with your face?"

"Measles," said Hart shortly. "I brought measles to Captain Halliman's fort. I also brought a dispatch, but it wasn't of much importance. Sit down, Rod, and prepare to be quarantined."

They all laughed.

"General Scott's bad luck, I call the measles," said the captain. "Half the army's got them, I understand—just in time for the spring campaign."

All this was news to Rod. Although John Fox had told him about General Scott's appointment and plan for a campaign, he had only the Indians' scanty news about armies marching to keep him posted on military movements.

Hart became serious. "Captain, I know you're anxious to talk with Rod. From the looks of his clothes and the length of his hair, he hasn't been near civilization for sometime. How about it, Rod?"

"No, sir, I haven't. I do have some news, though."

"First, let's find out if you're hungry," said the captain kindly.

"Yes, sir."

The captain ordered a man to get Rod some pork and hard-bread. While the pork was being cooked, he took the boy to the opposite end of the fort and they perched together on a sack of corn, away from the sick men.

"I want to know where you came from, what you know about the movements of General Scott's armies, and any information you may have about the Indians."

Rod told him his story, including the information he had learned about troops marching from both east and west.

"That western column would be Colonel Lindsay's, coming from Fort Brooke," said the captain thoughtfully. "They were to make a juncture with columns led by General Clinch and General Eustis, somewhere up the Withlacoochee. General Scott has planned a neat little trap for the Indians—if they'll only stay where they were six weeks ago."

"Yes, sir."

"Our troops have moved toward the cove in a three-pronged pincer," the captain continued. "If the Indians are there, General Scott should be able to force a decisive battle."

"Yes, sir," agreed Rod, "only they won't be there. They're going southwest, sir. They're running away. I think they'll settle much farther down the peninsula."

"That's the worst of it," concurred the officer sadly. "They seem to be slipping through the net. But did you hear anything about General Clinch's troops, marching from Fort Drane?"

"An Indian runner said they were ready to march—that was some time ago."

"And General Eustis' troops had left the East Coast and crossed the St. Johns River?"

"I guess it was General Eustis' troops they talked about."

"Then we're bound to hear from them soon," said the captain briskly. "They seem to have started on schedule and we have to figure on a little delay." Rod noticed he seemed relieved. "I may as well tell you, Rod," he added, "that our detachment is here to guard a large store of corn, intended for the various columns when they converge along the river. It was thought the fighting might continue for a long time and extra rations be needed."

"I see, sir."

"Major McLemore, our commander, has gone out to report our establishment of the garrison and to bring relief to our men."

"Yes, sir."

"Frankly, I hoped you were bringing word from General Scott."

"I'm sorry, sir."

The captain continued speaking, worriedly now. "The blockhouse is isolated and our garrison very small. Even if we build defenses, we may not be able to hold them. I should like to make contact with one wing of the army."

"Yes, sir. If there's anything I can do, sir, I'll be glad to."

"Thanks, Rod. I may call on you. Maybe I'm impatient. This is a waiting assignment."

"Could I take a message?"

"Not yet. But I'll remember your offer. You and Hart Whitley are my two scouts. The rest of my men are from farther north. They're unfamiliar with this country."

"Yes, sir."

The captain rose. "When you're through eating, Rod, get

some rest. Better bunk down here, though, away from those men with the measles."

Rod nodded. But he looked surreptitiously toward the other end of the fort, where Hart Whitley lay quietly. If a scout as good as Hart could get the measles, so could anyone else. "Half the army's got them," Captain Halliman had said.

It didn't sound good to Rod.

Chapter XI

Signal Shot

"Major McLemore sought the service by private letter to the undersigned, stating that he had on the Suwannee a boat suitable for the expedition and supplies which he could bring with him."

—Colonel Gadsden in a deposition
read at trial of General Scott

Two weeks passed quietly, without any sign of Indians or word from any of the three columns. Hart Whitley recovered from the measles and Rod caught them. He had a light case and hardly knew he was sick.

The other men weren't so lucky. One by one they came down with a high fever, followed by the measles rash. Several of them had bad aftereffects, and a husky young man named Hawkins contracted pneumonia. But Hart Whitley brought him through it with a weird concoction of herbs.

The men who slept near Hawkins hated to hear his phlegmy coughing in the night, so near their own blanket beds, and guard duty became very popular. The big fire and the cold, sweet air spiced with wood smoke were a welcome change.

"Nice place to store food—in a pesthouse!" observed Captain Halliman as Hart came in from guard duty one evening. But he laughed as he said it, for no officer would ask his men to sleep outside in Indian country.

117

"Looks as if you ought to be hearing from Major Mc-Lemore," remarked Hart, chewing moodily on a grass stem. "It's well past the time your men were to stay here."

Halliman shifted restlessly. "I can hardly believe it," he said, "but General Scott's three columns must have missed us completely—or else didn't get this far. We haven't heard a single shot, or seen any Indian activity. Do you suppose they could have fought a major engagement somewhere farther east?"

"It's possible," said Hart, "but I doubt it. The Indians don't want a major battle."

"Then what do you think has happened?"

"Just between you and me," Hart confided, "I doubt if Scott could march an army across Florida in the time he allowed himself. The men'll have to chop roadways, build bridges across streams, and drag supply wagons through worse mud than General Scott has ever seen up north. Now, as I understand it, the general's volunteers are in the war for only three months. They're coming from Georgia, the Carolinas, Alabama, Louisiana and nobody knows where else. By the time they're assembled, drilled and marched across the Territory, the enlistment period is over—and where's the time to fight? Don't you agree, Captain?"

"That's going to be one difficulty, no doubt," said the captain gloomily.

"Another thing," Hart went on, "is the way the Indians can run rings around Scott's slow-moving columns. If the warriors don't want to fight, they won't. And if the Seminole villages have moved south, there won't be any need to make a stand."

"I hope you're wrong."

"Know what I think?" continued Hart. "I think the Scott campaign is over. I'll bet you my best pair of moccasins that the whole thing fizzled. If the armies aren't up here now, trying to root out some Indians, they must have gone back to their starting places. That's my guess, anyhow."

The captain looked glummer than ever. "I don't like to think of where that leaves us."

"It leaves us holding the sack—or rather a thousand bushels of corn, with no army to eat it. And we don't dare let the Indians capture the supply."

There was a long silence, as Captain Halliman digested the meaning of Hart's talk.

"I hope you're wrong," he said again.

"I hope so, too."

"But what's happened to the Indian warriors? Why haven't we seen any?"

"There'll be some around eventually. They just haven't found us yet."

Captain Halliman groaned, then his face brightened. "We still have Major McLemore to count on. He'll get relief to us if anyone can."

But in spite of the captain's hopeful talk, two more days went by without word from the absent major. The men were uneasy, wondering what was wrong. Among them the rumor spread that McLemore had been taken prisoner by the Indians and could not return to the blockhouse. To quiet the garrison, Captain Halliman put them to clearing more ground and extending the blockade.

All during the second day, Hart seemed uneasy, and in late afternoon he kept looking toward the hammock. Rod, too, was listening to sounds that came from beyond the silent, moss-hung oaks. The mocking bird there would sing for a time. Then his voluble bird chatter would be repeated on the other side of the clearing. It happened not once but several times.

"They've discovered us," said Hart tersely to Rod. "Guess I better tell the captain."

He went into the blockhouse and a moment later Halliman came to the door. He shouted an order. The men had put up their axes a short time before and now were strung up and down the bank of the river, some fishing, some skipping stones, some watching a wrestling match. They came quickly to attention, faces bewildered. At once they fell into double file as ordered.

"Into the blockhouse! Forward, march!"

The men marched in close, disciplined lines. Inside, questions popped like fireworks. "What's up? Indians?" "Who saw 'em?" "Where?"

Captain Halliman spoke: "Men, our scout—Hart Whitley—believes the woods are filled with Indians. We may expect an attack now, or maybe hours from now. Check your guns and find your posts."

The men cheered. Here was action, after the long period of waiting. They were ready.

"Let me at 'em!" cried a tall fellow named Searles, whose wiry black beard and heavy eyebrows gave him a fierce expression. "I come down here to fight Indians, and I ain't going home without I get a scalp, leastways a scalp lock!"

The rest laughed loudly, for all approved of these sentiments.

To their disappointment no attack came. The hammock remained shadowy and mysterious, without a sign of Indians. Even the bird calls ceased. Hart took a bit of "joshing" from one of the men, who suggested he "seen a rabbit jump or maybe a deer peek out."

"Indians are never in a hurry," Hart remarked dryly.

That night the captain doubled his guard, sending them into the fringes of the hammock. Some of the men did not seem eager for duty that night; others—among them Searles—clamored to go.

"All right, Searles, step up," said the captain.

"Thank ye, sir," replied the recruit, grinning wickedly through his beard.

"You may have a chance to get that scalp."

"That's what I hope, sir."

Rod slept badly that night. Whether he was waiting for a war whoop, suffering from a hornet sting of the day before, or was just too uncomfortable, he didn't know. Some flying cockroaches had got through the netting into the blockhouse, and they kept whirring over Rod's head, or landing with a plunk against the log walls. Since the rains, clouds of huge mosquitoes—known as gallinippers—had plagued the men. By day the insects hung in the shady hammock, afraid of the sun's wilting heat; but at night they invaded the fort. Hundreds drifted in whenever a man entered or left the structure, and their buzzing filled the room. The welts they raised itched as badly as the recent measles rash.

For a time Rod slapped at them, but at last he dozed off. He woke at the moaning of screech owls. Was it owls or Indians? He could not tell.

He turned over, hurt his hornet sting and turned back again. Morning soon would be here. The luminous half-light of dawn showed through the smoke vent and door. He closed his eyes but was jerked wide awake by a rifle shot.

He jumped to his feet. Men everywhere were up, grabbing their guns. Another shot sounded, then a third.

It's the sentries, thought Rod. The Indians would shoot a volley and then whoop.

Already men were standing at the loopholes of the blockhouse. Although he had no gun, Rod joined them. Through a chink in the wall he could see sentries tearing across the clearing, in full flight. Four on his side of the building. In the half-light he could not identify them. They reached the fort, burst through the door.

"Indians—I saw them!" panted the first.

"Me, too."

Captain Halliman scanned the men. There were nine of them. "Where's Searles?" he asked abruptly.

No one knew. Searles was the only guard who had not come in.

"Report, Carson, what you saw," said the captain sternly.

Silas Carson, a quiet, steady young man, spoke: "I saw a dark shadow behind a tree. It was back inside the hammock—couldn't have been a sentry. I hailed it and got no answer. The shadow moved again, so I fired into the air—like you said, for a signal."

"Malloy?"

"I seen them for sure!" cried the excitable Irishman. "Same as Carson—only five or six! I fired, sir, as instructed."

"Anybody else fire? There were three shots."

The others had not discharged their guns but had run in when they heard the warning signal. Captain Halliman turned to the men at the loopholes. His voice was steady.

"Hold your fire, men. We may be attacked at any moment. Let's give them a volley if they try to cross the clearing. And be sure you let Searles come in unharmed."

"Maybe I'd better go after him," said Hart Whitley as he put his shot pouch over his shoulder.

"No, Whitley. I have a job for you—later. Besides, Searles may be hiding, or stalking Indians on his own. He was anxious for a scalp. If he's alive, he'll try to come in."

"Yes, sir," agreed Hart.

The woods was unnaturally still as the sky lightened. The whippoorwills had stopped calling, and the usual bird twitter of morning was absent.

"Looks as if there might be a lot of the savages this time," the captain remarked to Hart. "What do you think?"

"It looks very much like it."

The silver-gray of morning stole across the forest, dimming the stars and outlining the moss on the oak trees of the hammock. As the sun rose from behind the eastern curve of the earth, the forest grew rosy, and the night cold gave way to a creeping warmth.

"Where are they?" asked Captain Halliman, puzzled. "I thought they liked to attack at dawn."

"They do," replied Hart. "But they like best to attack when no one is expecting them."

"I see."

The men had hardly stopped talking when a low, groaning sound came from the hammock. It rose, fell and rose again, like someone in great pain. Some of the men half turned away from their posts, looking to the captain for orders.

"What do you think, Whitley?" asked the captain. "Is it the real thing? Could it be Searles?"

Hart shrugged. "I'd say no. But I may be wrong. What's your guess, Rod?"

Rod had been peeking through the slit between the logs. "I don't know, sir," he said, feeling proud that Hart had asked his opinion. "The noise is right in the spot where Searles was patrolling, near the river. But it might be a bit too loud for a hurt man. And I don't know why he didn't groan before."

"Good thinking, Rod," Hart praised him. "We've heard no gun since the sentries fired—and those signals were aimed into the air. That third shot is the only one unaccounted for—it might have wounded Searles. But if that did strike him, why didn't he groan before, as Rod says?"

"All right, men," said the captain briskly. "Watch your loopholes. We'll assume the sound is Indians."

"Unless," added Hart slowly, "he might have been shot with a bow and arrow—or stabbed . . ."

He was interrupted by a new outbreak of groans. This time they reached an agonized crescendo and were followed by a faint "Help!" The men moved uneasily. One of them drew his gun from a loophole and came over to Captain Halliman. He squared his shoulders and saluted.

"I'd like to go out there, sir. Searles was a special friend of mine. I'd rather not stay here if he was yellin' for help."

"It's probably Indians," the officer reminded him.

"Yes, sir. But in case it's really Searles . . ."

"You may go."

"Thank you, sir."

The volunteer cocked his rifle and moved toward the door. He was a small, bandy-legged fellow named Tommy Potts, whose eyes were starkly serious. Rod had thought him funny-looking before, but now he felt a strong liking for the nervy little man.

Tommy was let softly out the door of the blockhouse. Gun in hand, he walked boldly around the log structure and started across the clearing in the direction of the sounds. They had mellowed now, almost stopped.

Rod watched through his chink, holding his breath. His admiration was strong for Tom Potts. It was good to have a friend like that, no matter how undersized and skinny-legged.

Tom was halfway across the clearing now. The sun peered above the trees, ready to flood the clearing with pale morning rays. It shone on Tom's shapeless, slept-in uniform. It cast his elongated shadow over the tree stumps and fresh chips of the clearing.

The groans had stopped. Tom was almost to the trees. Like a sudden clap of summer thunder, a rifle sounded from the hammock. Then many rifles. Potts stopped short, wheeled sharply and ran like a madman. A shout rang out from the blockhouse. Above it rose Captain Halliman's brusque, "Fire!"

A shattering volley came from the blockhouse, as every man picked a shadow in the hammock and strove to pierce it with a leaden ball. But all left a lane of safety for gallant Tom Potts.

He was halfway to the fort now, running with head down, a bit of human life that defied the bullets around him.

He drew close, began to weave. "He's hit!" groaned several of the men. Still the running figure came on.

Ten feet from the blockhouse he stumbled and fell. But Hart Whitley threw open the fort door, ran out and dragged him inside.

Tommy lay on the floor, wordless, but looking up at Hart with gratitude in his eyes. He was bleeding from a wound in the shoulder. The men cheered him, even as they rammed new bullets into their guns.

Hart bent over him. "Lucky Tom Potts," he said softly, looking at the soldier's bullet-torn clothing. "Your uniform's slashed to ribbons, but all you got was a ball in the shoulder. It'll keep you from shooting for a while, but you'll get well. Get my kit, Rod."

Rod ran to get the medicine kit, and Hart set to work extracting the bullet. It had cut a deep tunnel in the flesh. He was cleansing the torn place, Tom Potts sweating and twisting but not saying a word, when there came a savage rhythmic shouting from the hammock.

"Pow-pow-pow-pow woo loo—woo loo—pow-pow-pow woo loo . . ."

"Up men! All at your places!" ordered the captain briskly.

Most of the men were still at the loopholes. They cocked their rifles and gripped them tighter, squinting along their barrels. Others hurried to their places. All were eager. The attack had come!

"Pow-pow-pow woo loo loo loo . . ."

A volley of rifle bullets struck the stockade, thudding against its logs and knocking off a splinter here and there. One ball struck through the slit where Rod had been peeking not five minutes before, z-zinged across the blockhouse and buried itself in the opposite wall.

"Pow-pow-pow woo loo loo loo!"

"Pick them off, fellows," ordered Captain Halliman.

Rod wished desperately that he had a gun, so he could take part in the fight. He was just going to ask for Tom Potts' when Hart called to him.

"Finish this, will you, Rod? I've got to see what's doing." He indicated Tom Potts' bandage.

Hart stepped to a loophole, and Rod began tying the ends of the cloth. "May I use your gun, Tom?" he asked eagerly. "I'm a good shot!"

"Sure, boy," said Tom, unsmiling. "Take it and welcome."

"Thanks, sir."

Rod finished dressing the wound and took up the weapon. Loopholes were scarce, so he stuck the gun barrel through the slit he had used before. Out beyond the clearing, in the hammock, he could sight the Indians, plainly enough. They were everywhere, behind every tree. As far as he could see, there were Indians—hundreds of them.

Where the sun struck slantwise into the deep woods, he glimpsed their brilliant shirts and red war paint. The bobbing of feathers, the gleam of a silver breast plate, told him just where they fought. There was one, standing behind a tree, while a comrade lay on the ground, both using the same tree for cover. A tall warrior stepped out, deliberately took aim and fired, as if he scorned shelter. Another spat his bullet into the gun muzzle, bumped it hard against the ground, preparing to shoot.

"Pow-wow woo loo woo loo!" The terrifying yell rose and fell as the firing continued.

The men in the blockhouse aimed carefully and few bullets were wasted. Only a little spilled powder showed the undercurrent of excitement. Now and then an overbold Indian drew more than one ball. When that had happened two or three times, the men began calling to one another. "He's mine—that

fellow with the yellow shirt" or "that one with the red feather!"
so that no ammunition would be lost.

Captain Halliman directed the fight, passing along from man
to man, inside the smoky, noisy blockhouse. His voice steadied
Rod. "Keep firing, boys. But if they start across the clearing,
hold your ball till they're close. Then make it a sure shot."

For two hours the battle continued. Indian war whoops
sawed against the nerves, but the men held firm. The little fort
grew hot and filled with powder smoke. Several men were
wounded, but none seriously. Then, as suddenly as they had
come, the Indians were gone. Not so much as a blanket corner
or a bright plume showed inside the hammock.

The men looked to their captain. "They're gone for a while,"
he said. "Let every other man stay at his loophole till we're
sure. The rest of you open up some more powder and clean
away what's been spilled. You boys fought well and I'm proud
of you."

The sun rose to noon and the Indians did not return. The
captain posted a few lookouts and sent out a detachment to
look for Searles. The others were told to eat. Most of them
grabbed up some hardbread and washed it down with water,
saying that was enough. Nobody dared light a fire inside the
fort, with so much spilled powder around. Besides, the heat was
already oppressive.

The afternoon was painfully long. The detachment came
back saying there was no sign of the missing soldier. The
blockhouse became hotter than ever and the men sick and bored
with their imprisonment, though none of them complained.
Toward evening, three of them volunteered to build a cook
fire outside, in the shelter of the partially finished stockade.

The captain agreed. When the fire had been started, coffee
boiled, and panbread put over the coals along with some pork,
the rest of the company began drifting out of the fort. Nothing
had happened to the three volunteers, and it looked as if the

coast was clear. The woods were quiet, whippoorwills were starting to call, and a bat swooped across the clearing.

"If this keeps up we'll have to build a better stockade," said Captain Halliman to Hart and Rod, as the three of them sat outside the building, leaning against its logs.

"I'm afraid it will keep up," said Hart thoughtfully.

"Me, too," offered Rod. "They don't want us here—on the Withlacoochee. And if they know we're defending all that corn . . ."

Hart nodded emphatically. "They haven't had a chance to raise their crops," he observed. "They need this corn lots worse than the Army does."

Chapter XII

Surrounded

"It is more than possible that we may be detained
in that vicinity (the Withlacoochee Cove) many
days reconnoitering the hammocks and searching
for Indians in the jungles and thickets of that
country. If so, the supplies which you report you
can bring may prove of essential service."

—From a message of March 25, 1836, written by
Colonel Gadsden to Major McLemore

They found Searles' body, that same evening, far inside the
hammock. There were three bullets in it, besides innumerable
knife wounds. The crown of his scalp was gone, as well as his
gun, ammunition and gold wedding ring.

Some of the men were awed and silent at the news; others
were loudly angry. Corporal Jones, who had been raised near
an Indian village and steadfastly insisted there were "both
good and bad Indians," forgot his philosophy and shot his gun
into the hammock, cursing all the tribes and calling them
"animals."

Tom Potts, when told, said nothing but turned his face to
the wall.

Although these men were trained to stern discipline and
fighting, they were more sobered by this one death than by the
battle itself. Searles' brash bravery had not saved him. His

brawny six feet two, his coarse black beard and his wickedly gleaming eyes were just as dead as if he had been a mewling little coward.

They buried him after dark near the edge of the clearing, and Captain Halliman said a short prayer over his grave: "Dear Lord, receive this brave soldier into the kingdom of Heaven. Amen."

That night, and every night thereafter, the guard was tripled. In the daytime no one was permitted to leave the blockhouse, except to get water from the river. The loopholes were always well-manned. In the hammock, Indians came and went, attacking many times. Their numbers increased, and Captain Halliman estimated there were eight hundred or more besieging the forty men of his command. The warriors were wary, having suffered many casualties to every one inflicted on the soldiers.

The men who had been most eager to receive word from Major McLemore drifted into a fatalistic belief that no orders were coming. It was now many days past the time they had expected relief. Lack of a message from the Army persuaded them that Clinch's column had already joined those of Eustis and Lindsay at Tampa Bay, without ever calling upon the garrison for its corn.

Worst development of all was the shortage of food. Their bacon and hardbread were gone; the coffee, although stretched along cautiously to the last bean, was gone too. There was nothing to eat except the huge store of corn they had been brought to defend.

They pounded it fine, mixed it with water and baked it in a frying pan as a cake. They mixed a coarser version of it with water and boiled it over the fire as mush. They parched it and made parched-corn coffee. Sometimes they just ate it as it was.

Within four or five days they all hated corn and swore they would never eat it again when they got back to civilization.

Rod chafed at the diet. He wanted to go into the forest and

shoot game, but Captain Halliman forbade him to cross the clearing. Hart, too, sternly warned him to stay in or near the blockhouse.

Tom Potts said, "Think of the day we buried Searles and you won't want to hunt in the hammock."

Rod agreed they were right. Still, he had a strong urge to shoot a deer—or even a couple of rabbits—to break the monotony of eating corn. Too, he suffered more than the others from the crowded state of the garrison. He was used to lots of elbow room, and here he had none. All day his ears were assailed by human talk, his eyes smarted from gunpowder fumes or smoke, and at night he woke to snoring and the smell of human sweat and wounds.

Slowly resolution came to him. He would slip away some night, stay outside a whole day and return the next evening, after dark. There had been no sign of Indians for two days, and he had a hunch there would be none for a time. His act would be disobedience, and subject to reproof, but if he brought in a deer he knew the men would cheer him.

Next day, while Rod was thinking out ways to make his escape, the captain ordered twelve men into the pine grove to the east. They were to cut logs and roll them toward the blockhouse. Others would extend the stockade, so that troops could venture out of the fort without being shot down.

It was a dangerous venture and the captain asked for volunteers, announcing that he himself would be one of the party.

Soon the detachment was in the grove, their axes swinging. Rod watched them from the log building, where he and other men stood at the loopholes. Rod now had a gun of his own, salvaged from a dead soldier, and he had taken more than one shot at the red-painted warriors.

In a short time eight trees were felled and their branches lopped off. As the ninth tree crashed, there came a volley of rifle shots, then a loud whoop from the hammock. Two men dropped among the pine boughs and lay still. A third fell, struggled to his knees and tried to rise. A fourth staggered toward the blockhouse.

The others grabbed their guns. Obeying Captain Halliman's crisp orders, some formed a half-circle around the wounded, while others helped them toward the fort. Backing slowly away from the woods, the riflemen shot and reloaded as they moved.

From his place at a loophole in the loghouse, Rod peered sharply toward the forest, found a shadowy Indian figure and groaned as it disappeared before he could aim and fire.

Every soldier on that side of the fort was trying to pick off an Indian, and there were few shots from the enemy as the detachment struggled to shelter. Captain Halliman, his sword flashing in the sun, was dragging a wounded man by the shoulders. In the hammock a plumed figure in a yellow shirt inched from behind a tree, aiming his rifle. Rod gripped his gun, sighted and fired.

He was too late. The Indian's weapon groaned, its bullet burned across the clearing. Captain Halliman stumbled and fell. He tried to get up, but could not. Two men from the blockhouse ran out to bring him in.

Something caught in Rod's throat. He poured out powder with a trembling hand, slammed a ball into his gun, flicked more powder into the pan and slid his gun through a loophole again. But when he looked for the Indian with the yellow shirt, the man was gone. There were others—lots of them—and more appearing every minute along the fringes of the hammock. Rod saw a pointing gun and aimed at its owner.

Behind him he could hear the detachment entering the fort. His name was called. Hastily he squeezed the trigger and sent the ball into the hammock. Without waiting to see if he had killed an Indian, he turned to Hart.

"Yes, sir."

"Give me a hand with these wounded. Lay them along the wall."

"Yes, sir."

Rod took the legs and Hart the shoulders of a soldier named Canaday and laid him close to the logs on the river side of the fort. The man was bleeding hard from a chest wound.

"Tend to him first," Hart instructed. "He and the captain are the worst. Do exactly as I tell you, Rod."

"Yes, sir."

"Put this swab over the bullet hole and prop him up a bit. Give him a swallow or two of this." He handed over some cotton and a small vial.

Rod turned to the man and laid the cotton across his wound. It soaked through in an instant, so Rod drew the man's shirt into a wad and laid it over the puncture. Canaday was as white as foolscap, but conscious and able to grin in a shamefaced way. Rod raised the man's shoulders and stuffed a blanket under them. With unsteady hands, he poured a few drops from the vial into the man's mouth. The medicine seemed to help, and Canaday murmured, "Good lad."

Rod had done everything Hart told him, so he turned to the next soldier, swabbed his wound and tried to make him comfortable. "You're lucky," the boy said, at sight of the clean tunnel through the flesh of the man's thigh.

"I sure am," the fellow agreed.

Canaday was trying to call. His voice had a strange bubbling in it. Sensing disaster, Rod whirled toward the man, swabbed away the blood on his lips. But more came.

"Hart!" called the boy.

Hart left the captain at once and bent over Rod's patient. He shook his head. "There's nothing to help him," he said. "Stay with him, though. Pray for him."

When Hart had gone, Rod sat beside Canaday, wondering what he could say. He had never prayed with a dying man—

that was work for ministers—and he did not know what words
to use. At last, as the man's breath seemed almost gone, he
knew he must speak.

Suddenly he recalled what Captain Halliman had said over
Searles' grave, and he repeated it: "Dear Lord, receive this brave
soldier into the kingdom of Heaven. Amen." When he finished,
he was scared. Maybe he had said it too soon; maybe it was
only a prayer for burying.

But Canaday did not act as if he had heard. Rod felt of his
wrist and could find no pulse. He tried to give him more medicine, but Canaday would not open his lips.

For an hour he watched beside the man, moving away sometimes to see to the others, but staying mostly with Canaday as
he saw the man's strength ebbing out of him. His skin had
turned cold, and now, when Rod listened to his heart, he could
hear no beat.

"Hart!" he called again.

His call brought the scout. Hart examined the man briefly.
"He's gone," he said. "Take your gun and get back into the
fight."

Rod swallowed hard and his knees trembled. The cold hand
of death had reached out and taken Canaday right from under
his hands. But he shut out his fear, found his rifle and took his
place at a loophole.

He was shocked at sight of the woods beyond. The hammock
was bristling with warriors—more than ever before. Bright
shirts, blankets and plumes were everywhere. Even the pine
grove had been invaded, and there were rifle barrels sticking
above the logs which the soldiers had just cut.

A volley sounded, and the war whoop that followed rang in
waves across the hammock. It had a volume and thunder such
as Rod had never heard.

Suddenly anger possessed him. He fired, reloaded, and fired
again, as fast as his haste-clumsy fingers could pour out the

powder and ram in the ball. He saw a brave fall and believed it was by his own bullet.

The shooting settled down to a ragged exchange. Shots spanged against the logs of the blockhouse like chunks of hail. Their noise was answered by the deep-throated rifles of the soldiers. Smoke floated thickly inside the enclosure and drifted out the fire hole above.

Lieutenant Walker, who was now in command, paced back and forth behind the men, stopping to look toward the hammock, frowning, pressing his lips together. Suddenly he shouted: "Hold fire! They're going to charge!"

For the first time, Rod noticed that the woods were silent. There were no yells, no rifle shots.

"Don't shoot unless you can kill!" cautioned the lieutenant sternly.

The men finished loading and waited. In a few seconds the charge began. Hundreds of Indians swarmed from behind the trees and started across the clearing.

"Hold fire!" cried the officer, from his place at a loophole.

Rod swallowed nervously as the Indians advanced. He could see the savage rage of their faces, the red and black war paint, the plumes and scalp locks streaming back from their heads. He found it hard not to shoot.

"Ready, men!" called the lieutenant. "Aim! Fire!"

Every man of the garrison squeezed his gun trigger. There was a stumbling all along the enemy line. Some of the braves sank to their knees, others fell and lay still. The remainder faltered.

With awkward haste, Rod reloaded. Feverishly he poured powder into the muzzle and dropped in a ball, thumping the butt of the gun against the dirt floor to make the bullet fall.

He stuck the weapon through his loophole, prepared to aim. To his amazement, the Indians were vanishing into the woods again.

"Hold fire!" shouted Lieutenant Walker.

Rod waited, his knees numb and shaking now that the charge had been repulsed. But he rested his gun in the loophole, ready to obey orders like the others.

The Indians did not appear again. They sifted back into the hammock and for a time the men thought they had gone. But just as everyone was beginning to relax, a soldier cried out that he had seen a flame arrow. Then they all saw them—streaking through the air like bright daylight meteors. One hit the smoke vent and fell down into the fort, where it was stamped out. Others dropped on the ground outside and flickered there harmlessly.

A crackling sound came from overhead. Rod looked up, saw a brown spot on the underside of the thatch. It widened, began to smoke. A glow came, then flames.

Rod ran for a bucketful of water, while Corporal Jones rolled a barrel under the fire spot and climbed onto it. When the boy came back with a brimming bucket, the corporal sloshed its contents onto the thatch. But already the flames had spread across the outer side of the roof. Before more water could be brought, they broke through again, and the blaze hissed and crackled in the dry palmetto.

The hole widened with incredible speed. As the fire roared higher, it released smoke and a stinging fog of heat into the log enclosure. Bits of burning thatch fell, igniting blankets and even the men's clothing.

There was a mad scramble to beat out these little fires, to cover the powder kegs and to find shelter from the intolerable heat. No one could see clearly. Eyes and throats smarted. Man shoved against man, all coughing, scared, half-strangled.

Someone flung open the door, and the soldiers streamed outside, only to dash back in as Indian bullets found them, bumping into other men who were struggling toward the open.

Almost as suddenly as it had come, the fire died. The entire thatch roof was gone, except the edges, which now burned slowly toward the log walls. Cool air came down into the fort. Smoke drifted out.

The confusion ended. Men crowded inside the fort, even without the lieutenant's order to "Get inside, everybody!" The door was barred. Men lined up at the loopholes and sighted into the hammock, mad for revenge.

But the Indians had vanished.

Lieutenant Walker conferred with Hart Whitley. "Are they gone? Or is this a trick?" he asked tautly.

"I think they're gone," replied Hart, "at least for the night. We left dead men out there, Lieutenant. The Indians'll take their scalps and paint them, then spend the night celebrating their victories.

"Thanks, Hart."

The officer at once ordered men to the river to get water. They were not fired on. But they came back to say the flatboat was gone.

"The flat!" repeated the lieutenant, his face gray.

"Yes, sir. Cut loose, sir. Nothin' left but a stub of rope."

Every soldier in the garrison was long-faced at the news. The flat had been their one boat—the means by which they had come upriver and the way they intended to get back. Now it was gone. Even if they got orders to leave, they couldn't. They were marooned.

There was little talk, and that of a glum sort, as the men chewed corn for their supper and kept a watch on the hammock. Hart Whitley, with Rod's help, cared for the wounded and bound up a number of minor cuts and burns left from the day's battle. Most of the gunshot victims were recovering, but the captain lay very still. His skin was an unhealthy blue-white.

When dark came, volunteers were called for to go into the hammock and bring back the bodies of the two men who had fallen while cutting logs.

Among the volunteers were Rod, Hart and Tom Potts. Rod was rejected at first but begged so hard to go that the lieutenant finally nodded. When four men had been chosen, the loopholes were manned to cover them, although little could be seen now by the light of stars and a cloud-drifted moon.

The dead were not hard to find. They lay just where they had fallen. But, as Hart had predicted, their scalps were gone. The bodies were brought back to the clearing and buried in the fort's small cemetery, where Searles lay. Lieutenant Walker said the prayer this time, speaking low, for the whole service had to be very quiet.

Hart and the lieutenant talked that night until their candle stub burned out. Hart told the young officer there were a thousand or more Indians in the attack that day. They would come again, he said. He urged the lieutenant to build boats and take his men down river.

"Hart, I'm only in command temporarily. Captain Halliman thought we should man the blockhouse. If we abandon the corn to the Indians, it may prolong the campaign in some vital field."

"Then let me go for help."

"Let's sleep on that. Captain Halliman may be better tomorrow. I'd rather leave the major decisions . . ."

Hart interrupted. "The captain won't be better tomorrow." His voice was harsh.

The lieutenant looked up sharply. "He will not?"

Hart's gray eyes did not blink. "He won't live the night out."

"You're sure?"

"He had a chance, but—he wasn't lucky."

Walker looked at the hard-packed dirt floor, bit his lip and did not answer.

"The decision must be yours," said Hart.

"I realize that. Still, I must sleep on it."

"Are you expecting Major McLemore?"

"Hardly—now."

"Then let me go tonight. I could slip out under this cloudy moon and swim down the river a ways. Once I'm past the Indians, I could get to help."

Lieutenant Walker thought a long time. At last he said, "With all respect to you, Whitley, I think it a poor time to send a scout anywhere. With a thousand Indians in the woods, you would be in extreme danger. Your message might never be delivered. If we had a canoe, so that you could slip down river in a hurry, I'd send you—now, tonight. But ordering a man out on foot is nearly certain death. Besides, I can use you here, to interpret the Indian strategy. Let's make it stronger—I need you."

That night Rod could not sleep. He lay in the roofless block-house, staring up at the mist-veiled stars, wondering what he could do to help. Although he admired Hart for his offer, he knew that Lieutenant Walker was right. This was a dangerous time to leave the fort.

He thought back to his own plan of sneaking away on a hunting expedition. Hunting now would be insane. But he could use the same plan to get outside, swim down the river and find the flat, in case it had lodged against the riverbank somewhere, or against a fallen tree. Such a feat would be worth the danger. And if something happened—well, the fort didn't need him as much as it did Hart.

The idea ran like hot fire through his veins. It possessed him. He could no longer lie still or stay inside the blockhouse.

The guard would be changing soon. When the relief left the fort, he would slip out too, under pretext of being on some errand for the lieutenant. If he were called back, he would come and take his punishment. If not . . .

Chapter XIII

Secret of the Cove

"The garrison were twenty-eight days without anything to eat but corn and nearly a month without any roof to shelter them."

—JOHN LEE WILLIAMS
in *Territory of Florida*

Rod was alone beside the river. He had walked out of the fort with the guards, carrying a bucket in each hand, as if he intended to get water. No one had called him back.

Quietly setting the buckets on the bank, he shucked off his jacket, laid it beside them and waded into the stream. At waist depth, he stooped down until the water covered his shoulders and shoved off with a hard leg push. In another instant, the current had seized him, was carrying him swiftly westward.

Now, for the first time, he felt afraid. The bank spun past with alarming speed. Soon he would be a long way from the fort. Its value as a refuge loomed big. His desire for adventure dwindled and he forgot his readiness to die for the garrison. Only the hope that he might find the flatboat kept him going.

A short distance downstream, he paddled into shallower water and looked around. Although he could see both shores dimly, there was no black shadow that could be the flatboat. He was surprised, for he had been positive it would be down river somewhere.

He swam with the current again. One mile, two, three. As he looked in vain for the boat, a sense of despair began to gnaw at him. He had broken the law to come out here, foolishly aspiring to be a hero. From inside the blockhouse it had looked easy. Now it seemed impossible.

His face burned against the cool water as he thought of how the men would laugh at him. They would say he was a crazy kid, not old enough for the Army.

The fourth mile reeled away without a sign of the boat, but he kept on from a desperate wish to succeed.

Ahead of him the sandbank tapered into a swampy cove. Hope still flickering, Rod decided to come ashore. The boat might have drifted into this little backwater.

He landed just above the cove, and crept quietly within the shadow of a cypress. From the bank he could look down into the narrow arm of water. It was choked with lily bonnets extending back some five hundred feet. But to his chagrin there was no flatboat lodged there.

His glance struck across the swamp, toward the opposite shore, and his heart gave a jump. There, where the riverbank resumed, were moored two Indian dugout canoes. Only their sterns showed beyond the deep shadow of the trees.

Greatly excited, Rod began to skirt the cove. In spite of his haste, he walked carefully. Indians might be near. He dared not warn them with a crackling twig, or by the plopping of frightened frogs into the water.

Something swooped down and almost struck him. He dodged back and crouched in the undergrowth. But it was only a bat, cutting dark arabesques through the night.

He was about to rise and go on when a flock of little screech owls farther back in the woods flew up in alarm and curved out over the cove, then back again. Pulse pounding, Rod dropped to the ground and lay there. He had not been near enough to those owls to frighten them. Someone else had done it.

He laid his ear to the earth and quaked at the soft treading echo he could hear. Indians—coming back from the hammock to the river—to get those canoes! In a minute they would pass him.

He backed into the undergrowth until the stiff fronds of a palmetto covered him and lay still, listening. The footsteps grew strong. Two or three men, he judged. They seemed to be coming straight toward him.

He heard a word in Seminole and understood it. One of the Indians had said, "Listen!"

They all stopped. For a long time there was silence. Rod wondered if his banging heart would vibrate against the earth, like the tread of their feet. Yet he was powerless to stop its panicky beat. At last a chuck-will's-widow began to call along the river, and a little owl moaned softly, again and again. The Seminole spoke, saying, "Go ahead."

The sound of feet grew loud against the ground. Leggings brushed the palmettos close to Rod. Then the Indians moved past, three of them, missing the boy by inches.

Rod lay there, sweating, long after they were gone, afraid to move or raise his head. The moon had edged higher in the sky and was casting a silver glow down into the palmetto. The night soon would be gone. He must get back to the fort. Yet he had not heard the Indians step into their canoes or paddle away.

He raised his head cautiously, but saw nothing. Slowly he stood up. His eyes sought the far bank of the river where the canoes had been. They were gone.

The night suddenly had a bitter flavor. He had been near to success, and it had evaded him. His luck had gone bad. Had he come an hour earlier he would have secured one of those canoes and been paddling toward the fort right now. Hart Whitley would have been proud, and the others would have thanked him. The garrison could have sent down river for help.

He started back around the cove, but halted suddenly, frightened by the reflection of the moon on some strange object among the lilies. It was silvery-gray, like a dead, bleached oak. But it was not fallen timber. It curved symmetrically, like a man-made object.

He moved toward it. With each slow step, more of the object came in sight. It stretched back into the lily bonnets, nearly hidden by them.

He came abreast of it, waded into the swamp and touched it with hands that trembled. He smiled to himself. Luck? He had been mistaken. His luck was tremendous.

Slowly he waded out of the swamp, drawing the cypress canoe after him. On the bank he examined it. Yes, it was his old canoe, all right. There were the holes made by the rocks of the rapids. That's why it had filled with water and stayed here all this time, half-submerged among the lilies.

With his finger tips he felt of the damage. Nothing that couldn't be mended. Bark and pitch would do the job.

He shoved the canoe back among the bonnets, carefully straightening them and drawing them over the boat, so that no one could see it had been moved. Then he turned toward the fort, his foot light against the trail.

Chapter XIV

Flight Down the River

> "When Major Read passed the mouth of the Withlacoochee (at the end of Scott's campaign) he discovered the flat cut in pieces. From this time it was generally supposed that the garrison were destroyed . . ."
>
> —JOHN LEE WILLIAMS
> in *Territory of Florida*

Tom Potts and Corporal Jones, Hart Whitley and Rod were chosen to go down river in the old canoe. Potts' wound was healed and he had proved his bravery. Corporal Jones, although of less rugged character, knew woodcraft and could speak Seminole.

Rod hid his proud excitement at being one of the party. Although he had received a stinging rebuke for leaving the fort without permission, he knew it did not come from the lieutenant's heart. And for the first time the men of the garrison were treating him like a grown man.

Although the four were anxious to start, they had to wait until Hart sneaked out of the blockhouse, repaired the boat and left it to dry. While they delayed, they whittled four light paddles to propel the craft.

The Indians did not come back and the hours were long. Although Captain Halliman had rallied during Rod's hours away from the fort, he lost strength the following day and suddenly his heart stopped beating. The men mourned him deeply, for they all loved him, and a feeling of black despair might have scuttled the morale of the garrison if it hadn't been for the expedition planned that evening.

Shortly after dark, the captain was buried beside his men, in the clearing. Then Rod, Hart and the others set off down river toward the hiding spot of the cypress canoe.

Tom Potts and Corporal Jones wore Indian clothes, taken from dead Seminoles. Rod and Hart already looked like Indians in their deerskin clothing. All members of the party painted their skins red as the Seminoles did and drew their long hair back into "scalp locks" pierced with feathers.

They found the dugout without trouble, still concealed in the lilies but ready to use. They carried it quietly to the river and lowered it into the water, laid the paddles and supplies in the bottom and climbed in.

The night was cool and with the recent clear weather the stars had become very bright. They pricked the river gently, making a path for the paddlers to follow. A line of sheltering trees along the right bank cast a thin black shadow.

The four had agreed not to speak until they were well down the river. They had agreed, also that, in case they became separated, the main party would continue on toward the Suwannee without waiting for the others. It was taken for granted that no man's life was to be considered as important as the relief of the garrison.

Three miles down river, they glimpsed a shred of flame in the woods. Rod's heart thumped wildly, but he obeyed Hart's whispered "Left," which guided them toward the far edge of the stream.

"Drift," Hart breathed again, as they drew near the light, and every paddle was raised and silent.

As Rod had guessed, the Indians had a camp here. The fire expanded as the boat came closer. He could see the logs of the

Seminole fire wheel and the Indians seated around the blaze, smoking their pipes. The two canoes he had noted earlier were shadowy shapes against the bank.

He sat with paddle motionless, just above the water, as the craft drew abreast of the camp. And suddenly a thought came that froze him with fear. Moving past, on the river this way, was like being a duck in a shooting gallery. If the Indians saw them—and they scarcely could miss—every man in the dugout would be knocked down like a wooden target.

The boat moved closer, until it was directly across from the camp. Rod stopped breathing. Maybe those Indians wouldn't look up from their comfortable fires and the solace of their pipes. Maybe the dugout would get through.

Foot by foot the boat drifted past the camp. It passed beyond the fire, beyond the two canoes along the bank. Ahead lay welcome darkness. Rod tensed his arms, ready to dip paddle again.

A startled shout ripped across the river. Then another. Against the glow of the fire, dark figures leaped to their feet.

"Paddle!" snapped Hart.

Rod plunged his blade into the water. He was aware that the others had done the same. They stroked in unison, and the boat slit the black surface, quivering with the power of their motion. Rod's fear vanished. He paddled with a swift rush of strength.

The braves seemed to melt into the darkness. Some of them stepped behind trees and raised rifles toward the boat. Several of them, concealed by the black tree shadows alongshore, were tumbling into the canoes.

Had they fired instantly, they must have killed every man in Hart's expedition. But they waited, confused for a moment by the men's Indian dress.

The boat was well past the camp before the first rifle roared. Its bullet slapped the water and was lost. Then came a second shot. Rod heard it whine overhead. A third went wide. But as the fourth sounded, wood splintered beside Rod's foot, and a thin stream of water began spouting into the canoe.

He dropped his paddle, snatched up a bailing bucket that lay in the bottom of the boat and caught the water, tossing it over the side and trying vainly to stop the leak with his free hand.

Ahead lay a bend in the river. Once around it, they would be out of sight and range.

"The boat's hit," he called to Hart.

"Can't stop," replied Hart. "How much water is she shipping?"

"Lots. I can't keep it out."

Tom Potts, sitting just back of Rod, spoke up: "I'll toss out a bag of corn."

Without pausing for an answer, he heaved a sack of corn into the air and let it splash into the water.

The boat rose a fraction of an inch. But it was enough. The bullet hole moved above the waterline and the water stopped coming in, except for an occasional spurt. Rod again took up his paddle.

They were passing the point. The night quiet of the river ahead was like a haven. But Hart spoiled their little victory by saying:

"Those canoes'll soon be around the point. Rod, get your rifle and step back into the stern. When they show up, give it to 'em."

Rod obeyed. As he crouched low in the back of the boat, rifle to shoulder, he wondered if the surge of the canoe would allow him an accurate shot. He tried to hold his sight on the dark elbow of shore, but it dipped and rose and the gun would not stay where he put it.

A thin gray splinter broke off the bend and drifted outward. Rod trained his sight against it. He did not look at the second canoe as it appeared. His sight bobbled against its target like a cork in a current.

"It's out of range," he called to Hart.

"Shoot anyway."

Rod held his gun steady and squeezed the trigger. The shot roared into the night. But the gray splinters still danced against the river.

"Try again," called Hart.

Rod reloaded. He noticed with surprise that his hands were shaking as he poured powder out of the horn. Again he aimed. The noise of his gun echoed with a ghostly din through the forest, but the canoes came on without wavering.

Hart turned to look back at their pursuers. "Try six fingers of powder," he said grimly.

Rod had never heard of shooting with that much powder, but he did as Hart said. When the gun was loaded, he raised it, tried to sight against the leading canoe. Again the light bobbing of his target angered him. But he steadied himself and squeezed the trigger.

The gun discharged with a terrific roar, kicking him backward. But he raised up, not caring, wondering only if those canoes had faltered.

They were still in the same place, still pointing ahead, like two dark-gray arrows.

"It worked," said Hart, chuckling.

Rod was puzzled. Then he saw that the canoes were dropping back. Their outlines grew smaller. When they had retreated a way, they stayed there, not gaining, not losing.

"Scared 'em," explained Hart. "Now paddle."

Rod laid down his gun, found his place in the dugout and slid his paddle into the river. The water in the boat had deepened and come up over his toes. As the craft filled, it dropped lower and lower.

"Water's coming in bad, Hart," he reported.

"That it is," added Tom Potts. "Got to lighten the boat again, sir."

"Go ahead."

Tom grabbed up a second sack of their precious food and sent it splashing into the river. Then he seized the pail and bailed out most of the water. The hole stopped spouting and only spurted water when the canoe rocked. But Tom was not satisfied. He took a bullet out of his shot pouch, wrapped it in a grease patch and stuffed the whole thing into the hole, stamping on it cautiously. It made a fine plug.

With an air of satisfaction he sat down again, took up his blade and plunged it into the water. With the four of them paddling again, the dugout skimmed ahead.

For a while they thought they were getting away from the Indian canoes. The gray marks on the river became smaller. But when the men tired, their pursuers crept in close.

"Well, we've powder and shot anyway," said Hart grimly. "And we're getting away from their camp. Wonder what they're planning."

"Can't figure it," mused the corporal. "I been ponderin' ever since they come after us."

"Got an idea, Tom?"

"Nope."

"Maybe we're running into a bigger camp down river," ventured Rod.

"Could be," agreed Hart. "Or maybe they just think they can outpaddle us."

"Look!" said Tom Potts suddenly.

The two Indian canoes were twice as big as before. They were catching up now—fast.

"Let's paddle," said Hart soberly.

Every man stroked fast and hard. Still the canoes drew closer. When their outlines were clear and sharp, Hart spoke to Rod:

"Get in the stern, Rod—and shoot. Keep shooting till you sink that first boat. They're in range."

Trembling with excitement, Rod resumed his place in the rear of the dugout. He had a good target now. But the importance of his job overwhelmed him. He had failed to make a hit the first time. Could he measure up now? The fear that he might not made him cold all over. Then he shook himself and gave a quiet laugh. He was a good shot. As good as Hart. If anyone could sink that boat, he could.

Taking steady aim, he fired. He heard a distant shattering of wood. Still the canoe came on, as fast as before.

He reloaded, shot a second time. This shot went wide.

When he raised his gun for the third time, he could see the shape of the Indians' naked shoulders and the bobbing of their feathers, silvered with moonlight. Choosing the light as a target, he fired again.

The first canoe seemed to drop back, and Rod knew he had made a hit. And in an instant he saw it edge toward the bank, as the other dugout shot past it.

A ribbon of fire unrolled in the second canoe; then came the deep groan of a gun. Another red ribbon was flung out and again came the same hollow, water-borne sound. In the prow of Rod's dugout the corporal gave a grunt and a strange gurgling. There was a thud as the craft listed heavily to one side.

Rod turned, saw the corporal lying across the bow, half in, half out of the boat. Hart was tugging at the man's body, trying to pull it back into the canoe.

"Keep paddling!" he shouted to Potts, who had started forward. "Rod, give 'em a ball!"

Rod needed no command. With hasty fingers he rammed in another load and raised his weapon. But that shot was never fired. In the bow, the corporal reared up with a loud groan, broke Hart's grip and slipped off into the water. The sudden shift of weight tipped the capricious boat. Men and provisions lurched sidewise, tilting it still farther. With scarcely a sound the canoe turned bottom up and dumped her crew.

Rod felt the water rise around him. It was warm from the sun of the day, but black and deep. Still clutching his rifle he went down and down. The current whirled him ahead, turning him this way and that.

At first he was surprised at the utter blackness around him. Then the tightness of his lungs warned that he must get air. He kicked his feet and stroked upward with his free hand. But the heavy rifle kept him from rising. His lungs began to pain. He could not reach the surface.

Knowing he must have air, he dropped the gun and at once rose slowly upward. His chest ached, but he broke through in time for a gasping breath.

When he had filled his lungs, he took a hasty look around. Tom Potts and Hart were a good hundred feet downstream, clinging to the overturned dugout. They seemed to be pushing it toward the far bank. Panic gripped Rod as he glanced in the other direction. The Indian canoe, manned by two braves, was whirling down toward him. It looked as big as the hull of a schooner.

Fear lent him strength for a straight, deep dive, and he paddled underwater toward the south bank. When finally he came up and looked around, the craft was past him. He took a breath or two and dived. As he disappeared, he felt something sting one foot.

This time he reached the shallows. He stayed under as long as he could, then stuck his head above the surface, clinging to a tree root in the river mud to keep his body beneath the water.

Far downstream, the Indian canoe was nearing the over-turned dugout. It looked as if Hart's rescue expedition was dead and done for.

One of the Indians leaned over the side of his craft, grasped something in the water and tried to raise it. Rod's stomach contracted—the corporal's body! Dead or living, they wanted a scalp, and they were fishing up their enemy to get one.

Rod's impulse was to shoot, but he had no gun. He could do nothing—only squirm with despair at his helplessness. He prayed that the corporal was dead, so that he would be spared this torture.

But the soldier was not dead. Even at this distance Rod could see him fighting, as if the dying officer still tried to conquer his enemies. The boat rocked violently. When it righted itself, it held only one Indian.

Angry triumph surged through Rod. The corporal was gone, but he had taken one of his slayers—and he had made a magnificent fight.

The lone warrior strove to control his canoe, which still rocked dangerously and had swung around in a crosscurrent. At last he could paddle and moved to where his comrade and the corporal had disappeared. But the water was smooth and star-flecked again.

Rod looked for his own overturned dugout. It was gone. In the moonlight the river looped cleanly between its banks. Rod strained to see what lay within the shadows of the forested riverbank. But there was nothing.

A warm, triumphant glow spread through him. Hart and Tom had got away. They were safe.

The lone Indian held his craft motionless in the current and looked around him. Then he turned upstream. Rod sank low in the water as he passed.

At last the canoe was almost out of sight. Rod crept ashore and into the brush, wondering how he could find Hart and Tom. If they were still on that other bank, he would risk a swim across the current to rejoin them. But if they had righted the canoe and slipped downstream, he was left behind.

He started to rise, felt a stab of pain and fell back onto the ground with a thud. Only then did he realize that something was the matter with his foot.

Its strong pulsing swept into his consciousness. He touched it. Although his whole body was wet from the river, this wetness of the foot was different. It was warm, and renewed itself, soaking his leggings at that spot. His fingers touched a deep gash.

He knew what had happened. That sting against his foot when he dived was the blow of a tomahawk.

Chapter XV

Ruther's Camp

"Seminoles ridiculed the United States troops, saying the march of the army was like that of the
gopher."

—A Lieutenant of the Left Wing
in *Sketch of the Seminole War*

The knowledge that he was wounded scared Rod. He was in a
bad spot. Hart and Tom Potts had gone—he would not have
kept them if he could—and he was miles from nowhere.

He remembered the instructions given at the blockhouse:
"No matter what happens, the main party will continue on
toward the Suwannee." It had sounded hard, then, but noble.
Now the corporal was dead—counted out—and perhaps Rod
himself had been counted out, too.

He forced himself to be calm, and at once saw that there was
only one sensible course—to rest and wait here until he could
travel. If he stayed alive till his foot was well, he might find
his way south to Tampa.

He crept back into the scrub and curled up under a palmetto,
putting his good leg beneath his wounded one and turning the
gash upward, to check the bleeding. A cobweb brushed his
hand, and he tore it down, wadded its sticky strands together
and laid it over the bloody place, remembering that Tom
Hadjo used cobwebs this way.

As soon as he stretched out, a drowsiness swept over him. He closed his eyes and slept.

When he opened them again it was almost noon. He was not strong, as he had hoped. The foot was throbbing and swollen.

The panic that he had felt before came back in a flood. He remembered stories he had heard, of death from such wounds. He looked closely at his leg, searching for the deadly red streak that meant the poison was spreading.

There were no red streaks. But as time passed and the throbbing grew worse, he determined to lance his swollen foot.

His knife was still in the sheath attached to his belt. He wiped it carefully on his shirt and punctured the puffy skin. Yellow fluid spurted out. He let it drip onto the forest floor and felt relief.

Now his mind, which had been pain-fogged, began to think in clear, sharp images, all neatly tied together in bundles of cause and effect. He thought of the men in the blockhouse and their long starvation, of kind Captain Halliman in his wilderness grave, and he hated the war that had caused these things.

He thought of Osceola's plea that the Treaty of Fort Moultrie be observed, instead of the new treaties of Payne's Landing and of Fort Gibson. He wondered how any white man could risk war for the dubious terms of the latter agreement.

He remembered brave Lieutenant Izzard and how red his blood had gleamed in the Withlacoochee shallows. And there was Searles and Corporal Jones and the soldier whom death had snatched away in the blockhouse, besides those others whom he had known. He multiplied them many times and a sickness grew in his stomach, and his breath began to come short, as if some great weight were suffocating him.

A long time he lay there. Gradually his revulsion tired him out, and he began to remember little homey incidents of his childhood: the dry-leaf smell of his cornhusk mattress, the warmth of the big fireplace on cold nights, and the hushed sound of his father's voice when he said grace before each meal. The memories comforted him, and in the cool of evening he again went to sleep.

The bird chirpings of morning woke him. He knew at once that he was better, even before he saw that the wound was shrunken and healing. A mounting optimism drew him to his feet and sent him hobbling around the woods, hunting for food.

He tweaked off the tips of a few unfolding fern fronds, chewed and swallowed them with mild relish. As he walked, a flock of quail whirred up directly in his path. His knife was in his hand, and he threw it. A bird fell to the ground.

Marveling at his good luck, he plucked the small fowl and found a fallen tree, where he could build a fire. Belatedly he rummaged in his pockets for flint and tinder. Again he was lucky, for they were still there, and the bit of scorched linen in the box felt dry to his touch.

He scooped a hole in the ground, put some dead grass and twigs in it and laid some larger wood close by. After a bit of coaxing he got a small blaze started and tossed on some bigger wood. He scattered it as soon as it caught, afraid he would create a column of smoke. Then he roasted the quail over a single burning stick.

It was a satisfying meal and it brought him fresh energy and hope. Even the huge turkeys and jellies of a Thanksgiving dinner had not pleased him as did this half-roasted little bird.

As he buried the bones, he began to scheme how he could spend the waiting period in accumulating food. On the theory that the stomach should be filled before the knapsack, he went to the river and hunted for crayfish or frogs. But he could find nothing.

When he thought his fire might be dying, he came back, replenished it and banked it carefully. Then he walked into the woods, looking for fresh tracks along old animal trails. To his joy, he discovered the broad, scuffing mark of a big gopher turtle and followed it to its hole. He was adept at trapping gophers, and he straightaway made a pit in front of the hole and covered it with grass and a dried palmetto leaf.

All day he continued his search for food, pausing frequently to rest the foot when it throbbed. In spite of his efforts, he found only a few berries.

Toward evening he dug up the quail bones and slashed a V-shaped piece from the carcass. It was a matter of minutes to carve a fishhook. When it was finished, he attached it to a long piece of vine, baited it with a fat grub and went back to the stream.

His first fling took the hook far out, beyond the shallows. As it dropped, the knotted vine slipped off the pole. Bait and bone fishhook vanished into deep water.

Rod was angry with himself for being careless. But he went back to the little heap of quail bones, whittled himself another hook and tried again. This time his luck was better. A fish snapped instantly and he drew in a twisting bream.

Triumphantly he carried it back to his fire, cleaned it and cooked it at once.

When the last bite of fish was gone, he lay down to sleep. Again he was optimistic. His energy had returned and he had plans for drying enough turtle meat over his fire to last the long trip south. He no longer worried about war and the reasons for it. His mind was occupied with the close, important details of keeping alive and getting almost a hundred miles through the untraveled territory to Tampa Bay. It would not be easy, with a lame foot and no gun. But he felt sure he could make it.

He woke when the sun rose and looked in the pit. The trap remained as he had laid it. Not a single blade of grass had been disturbed. The sight affected him deeply, snatching away

horse or even a wagon. Hoofprints were distinct in the soft soil.

Overjoyed with his find, Rod hurried along the path, wondering who traveled with horse and wagon this far up the peninsula. He had never heard of any settlement or even a single settler's cabin in this area.

There must be a camp near by, he figured, for no one would chop out a broad trail like this one unless he intended to use it over and over again.

For half an hour the boy followed the road toward the Gulf, sometimes angling a little southward, sometimes heading straight west. He thought happily of how he would drop in on a farmer's family, of their hospitable greetings and the fun of talking with people again. At last, when the wind freshened and took on a faintly salty smell, he saw a break ahead in the woods and beyond it the outlines of a cabin.

A doubt stabbed him. This could not be a farm. It was too near the Gulf, for one thing. Good soil for farming was not found on the Gulf beaches, or near salt water. This cabin, although built of logs and about the size of Rod's home, did not look like a farmhouse.

He stepped off the trail into the undergrowth and began working his way toward the cabin, thinking he would inspect it before making himself known.

In a few minutes he reached the clearing. It was unusually large, as if someone had expected to plant a big field of cotton or corn. But the stumps were still in the ground, and the soil between them was light-colored and poor, not good enough for crops. Through a grove of cabbage palms beyond the house he could see the white sand of a beach and beyond it the roll of gentle surf.

A strange setting, he thought. More like a loading station for boats, or a trading post. Stranger still was the tall stockade —as tall as any around the forts. It did not surround the log building but extended in back of it to enclose nearly half an acre.

Could Lindsay's troops have camped here and built this as a fort? he wondered. It was possible. Yet something told him this structure was not built for defense. The stockade suggested only one thing—a huge corral for horses or cattle.

Relieved at the thought, Rod looked for signs of the owner or his family. But the place seemed deserted.

Still uncertain and suspicious, Rod backed into the undergrowth again and worked his way toward the trail. Surely, if he waited along the entrance road, someone would come past, and he could give them a careful looking over. The timber was tall here and the vegetation thick; it would be easy to hide.

Overhead a woodpecker flashed past and sank his sharp beak into the bark of a pine. The sudden rat-a-tat startled Rod and he glanced upward. As he did so, his gaze caught and held against a tall oak. Someone had chopped out toe holds in the gray bark. And high up, in the tree's curving network of boughs, was a log platform with thatched roof. A lookout tree!

Rod hurried toward it and in a few minutes was climbing up. It was easy to reach the platform, and when he stood on it he had a clear view of the Gulf. There was a small natural harbor here, sheltered by arms of land on either side. And below him he could see the road as it wound through the forest and emerged in front of the cabin. Whoever came along that road could be inspected carefully from the tree—even shot down, he thought grimly, if the watcher were so inclined.

The big corral seemed to be empty. It contained nothing except a broad sandy floor. But in a tiny enclosure between cabin and corral, Rod looked down upon a small cannon. It was turned toward the Gulf, as if this might be the spot where trouble would start. At sight of it, Rod was more puzzled than ever.

He dropped his scrutiny of the cabin to examine the lookout platform. It was crude, made of logs nailed together on two crossbars. The thatch roof was carelessly done, and already the winds had blown part of it away. There was nothing else there, except a humpy bit of rotting canvas at shoulder height in the crotch of a limb. Rod looked at it curiously, lifted the canvas and peeked beneath.

He caught his breath at sight of the gleaming, brass-mounted telescope, lashed to the tree limb with strips of rawhide. It, too, was pointed toward the Gulf.

With a feeling of awe, he put his eye against the glass at the small end. He had never looked through such an instrument before, had only seen one of them on a boat, and could hardly believe they would help to see things far off.

To his astonishment, he seemed to swing out over the Gulf. Huge swells moved just below him, gulls planed within reach of his hand, and there, on the horizon, he could see a small schooner sailing north.

His glance wandered over the water and discovered nothing else. Wanting to look at the cabin below, he slit the thong that held the telescope and pointed the glass in the direction of the house. Now the cabin loomed close, and for the first time Rod observed that it was equipped with loopholes for muskets. He was not surprised, for the cannon had told him that these people feared someone or something.

He trained the telescope onto the corral and was startled at the sight of human footprints in the sand. A curious thought struck him. Could it be that this pen was for human beings? Were people being kept prisoner here? But he shrugged that off as being too fantastic.

He was still eying the cabin when he heard hoofbeats and voices along the road that led into the clearing. Hastily he laid the telescope on the platform and crouched beside it, not wanting to be seen.

The hoofbeats grew louder, and Rod's eyes clung to that part of the trail where the horses would appear. First came a gaudy roan, ridden by a stout little man in buckskins, and close behind plodded an Indian pony bearing a tall Negro.

Rod's blood turned cold. He had never once thought of Ruther in connection with this cabin and stockade. But now he reproached himself for being stupid. Ruther's "hide-out," some distance north of Tampa, had often been discussed in his presence. Although no one knew exactly where the cabin was, with its cannon and slavepens, folks at Fort Brooke talked about it in angry whispers, saying that Ruther never returned any of his captured slaves to their owners but sold them outright to the captain of a schooner and pocketed the money.

Here, then, was the hide-out, and the slavepen—and that boat on the horizon might even have been the schooner sailing away, since the pen was empty.

Hardly daring to breathe, Rod watched the two men dismount. Ruther went into the cabin, while the Negro turned the horses out to graze and carried in a load of wood. Soon a thin spiral of smoke drifted out of the chimney, and Rod fancied Big Dan'l was cooking supper.

The safest thing was to get away, Rod decided. He wanted nothing to do with Ruther or Dan'l, ever again. He stood up cautiously and was about to climb down the tree when he heard the loud bang of a gate. He ducked low and watched Dan'l as he entered the slavepen. To the boy's surprise, the Negro carried a bowl of food. Without a word or glance, he set it down inside the corral and went back into the cabin.

Rod had not noticed any dogs, or an animal of any kind, and now he watched to see what would come to be fed. It was several minutes before anything happened. Then a chain rattled and from the shelter of the southeast pickets, where he had been hidden from the telescope's eye, came a tall, thin Indian boy. He moved jerkily against the chains on his ankles, stood looking down at the food as if he hated it. Abruptly he stooped, picked up the bowl and wolfed the contents.

Rod stared, shocked. He grasped the telescope, raised it and adjusted the glass. For a long moment he peered through it, breathing hard. At last he laid it again on the log platform.

Yes, the boy was Shakochee. Shakochee, thin and dejected— half dead, probably, from starvation.

Stunned and unbelieving, Rod stood for a long time, adjusting his thoughts, letting the knowledge sink in that Shakochee was Ruther's prisoner. He could not understand, at first, how it had happened, for the boy feared Ruther and stayed out of his sight. How could the man have captured such a flitting woods' shadow?

Reluctantly, Rod realized that Shakochee's tribesmen might be responsible for this. Conviction struck him suddenly that Shakochee was here in place of himself. Those kegs of powder that the Indians needed—something or someone had to be traded for them. The old chief must have paid with Shakochee, as punishment for freeing Rod.

Now Rod was bound, as surely as if rawhide tied him to the slaver's pen. Here he must stay, to do what he could for his friend. For it was his turn again to help the Indian.

A wry smile lifted one corner of his mouth as he thought of his dull-bladed hunting knife. It was all he had against Ruther's guns, knives and small cannon.

For a long time he crouched in the tree, thinking what he could do. Shakochee had moved to the Gulf side of the stockade where the shadows were longest. Although Rod could not see his face clearly, the hunched-up knees and dejected shoulders told him how Shakochee felt. But he had not given up, Rod thought, in spite of the chains and the high stockade. He was waiting, not losing courage, but waiting, as men of his race were taught.

The sun turned a gaudy blood red as it dropped toward the

rim of the Gulf and sank into the water. For a while the clouds reflected its glow, then faded. Night began to blot out the lines of the forest.

The smoke from the cabin chimney dwindled to a crawling wisp and died away. As the last bit of color hung over the water an angry shout sounded from inside the hut. It was followed by a cry of fear from the Negro and a scream. Then came the snap of a whip and a grunt of pain.

Rod stiffened as blow after blow thudded against the quiet night. The grunts turned to sobs. Rod was glad he had not carved a lucky piece for Dan'l. No charm could help him now.

The whipping ended abruptly. The sobbing trailed off and the night was silent. The moon began to rise over the forest and cast its light onto the sandy floor of the slavepen. Rod could make out a shadow that was Shakochee, still sitting in the shelter of the pickets.

"I'll help him," Rod vowed fiercely to himself.

Although he had only a vague plan, he climbed down from the lookout tree and approached the stockade. He walked softly, for in spite of the gentle hush-hush of the rolling surf, sounds carried a long way.

The woods thinned, the surf grew louder. At last the pickets rose before Rod, taller than Big Dan'l.

Scarcely breathing, the boy circled the log wall to the Gulf side, where Shakochee sat. Through narrow slits between the logs he could see the Indian, a dark shadow against the paler gray of the pickets' shade. Rod came close, put his mouth against a slit and whispered, "Shakochee!"

The shadow stirred, but no answer came.

Rod called again: "Shakochee!"

This time the Indian turned. Rod could see the startled gleam of his eyes.

"Shakochee," he spoke again, with swift urgency. "It's Rod. I'm outside the pickets. Can you hear me?"

"Luckmaker!" came the whispered answer.

Rod whittled away a bit of the pickets' bark and made a hole big enough to pass his knife through. "Here—get those chains off your feet. I'll help you over the wall."

"Yes, Luckmaker," replied Shakochee softly.

He grasped the knife, wormed it through the chink and began work quietly on his ankle chains. Rod could hear the thin scratching of metal against metal as the Indian boy tried to pick the lock that imprisoned him.

It took a long time. Once Rod drew breath sharply as the back door of the cabin creaked and Dan'l came out into the small court where the cannon was set. Rod expected the stockade door to open, but it did not. Apparently the big fellow slept beside the weapon, for quiet followed and finally a gentle snore.

Rod could hardly believe his good luck. With Dan'l asleep, the escape would be twice as easy.

Rod wanted to speak to Shakochee, to tell him to turn the knife point in the lock keyhole, but he dared not make a sound. He could hear the steel faintly, still scratching against the chain.

Time stood agonizingly still, with only the Negro's snores and the gritty scraping of the knife to break the tension. Then came the soft quaver of a little screech owl at the edge of the clearing.

As the noise undulated through the clearing and died away, the back door of the cabin opened.

"Dan'l," came Ruther's voice, gruffly. "Take a look at the Indian."

"Yassuh," replied Dan'l, scrambling up from his sleep.

"That don't sound like an owl to me," grumbled the slaver.

"Nossuh."

"I'll look outside the stockade."

Rod's heart jumped. He would have to hide. But there was nothing on this sandy side of the pen that would conceal a rabbit. He leaped up and sped around the pickets in the direction of the woods, dodging stumps and leaping over long vines.

There was a shout from Dan'l, as he glimpsed the boy through the stockade. As Rod streaked across the moonlit open strip to the woods, he saw Ruther rounding the far end of the enclosure, gun in hand.

The man halted, flung weapon to shoulder and the rifle roared. Its whining ball passed over Rod's head. The boy plunged into the woods.

For a second he ran wildly, ploughing through saplings and vine-laden undergrowth until he could go no farther. The forest bound him with its rank creepers, foliage and seedling trunks. He tried to seek an animal trail, but in the darkness he found no way. Before him rose the notched trunk of the lookout tree. He sprang up it, climbed to the moon-grayed platform and lay flat, panting, hoping that Ruther would not guess he was here.

For a second he heard nothing. Then the crunch of underbrush told him the slaver had entered the wood. The noise came closer and closer. At last it stopped. Ruther's voice rose from directly below:

"Come down, you!"

Rod did not answer. He was not sure he could have moved his tongue anyway, for he was numb with shock. This was not like fighting with an army against another army, nor even the encounter of man against man in an even fight. He was trapped. Shakochee, too, was trapped—chained inside the stockade. At last Ruther had the two of them just where he wanted and his rage was running high.

From below came the click of the gun hammer, a small sound but an ominous one. Rod waited for the shot, but the voice came again:

"Climb down out o' there!"

Apparently Ruther had not recognized him, or he would

have called him by name. In the moonlight he had merely seen someone run across the clearing and climb into the lookout tree. Rod wondered feverishly if he could fool the man. Could he talk Seminole and make him think he had trapped an Indian and a possible slave? What could he say? And what weapon could he use against Ruther if his palaver did give him a reprieve?

Even as he hesitated, his mind a-skitter with schemes, the gun gave its shattering groan. There was a splintering of wood as the bullet bored through the log platform not two inches from Rod's waist, whipping into the oak leaves above.

The sound of the gun, terrifying as it was, wrought a change in Rod. His fright vanished, and he was once again the seasoned fighter under fire. He needed a weapon, and his arm reached for the telescope near by.

Keeping his shoulders low, so as not to make a target of himself, he extended the big glass to its full length and grasped it with both hands around the smaller end. It made a fair bludgeon.

Again the rifle roared, its ball thudding into the logs of the platform.

Knowing Ruther could not fire again until he had reloaded, Rod jumped to his feet, swung the telescope in a mighty half-circle and sent it flying into the woods below, straight toward his enemy.

Ruther saw it coming and jumped backward, so hastily that he tripped and fell sprawling. The telescope struck just below his feet, sank its brass lip into the dirt and remained standing rakishly upright.

Rod was dropping down the trunk of the oak, as fast as a monkey. He jumped the last fifteen feet and turned toward the slaver. Ruther had scrambled up and was clubbing his rifle. But no blow fell. A strange twanging noise filled the night. Rod caught a glimpse of something white streaking through the air, like a moonbeam stabbing obliquely into Sam Ruther's back.

Without a word, the slaver pitched forward and lay still in the scrub, his rifle still clutched loosely in his fists, the moonlight making a bright pattern on his buckskin-clad back. Above that back something quivered violently, slowed and finally bloomed like an exotic white flower in the quiet night.

Rod stared, unbelieving. Once before he had seen a white flower like this one, rising above his own father where he lay half-dead in the forest.

He glanced toward the woods' edge. A huge shadow was rising, stealing softly away, as if afraid of what it had done.

Hours later, Rod and Shakochee faced each other across a little campfire which they had built to roast venison and to dry out some jerky for the ride ahead. The meat they had gotten from the slaver's cabin, and they had boldly taken the two horses, for Dan'l was no place in sight.

It was the boys' first chance to talk, since their hasty flight. Although Ruther was dead, both Rod and Shakochee wanted to be a long way from his slavepens.

Near by, on the low limb of a boxwood, hung a drying scalp. Shakochee had taken it from his belt and put it there when they halted.

"It was Dan'l who shot the arrow," he explained, "but he did not kill. It was I, who came later. So I am entitled to the scalp."

Rod said nothing. It was the Seminole way, and he could not change it.

He opened his mouth to ask Shakochee how he had become Ruther's prisoner, but did not speak. If the Indian's own tribesmen had given him up, it would hurt to tell of it.

They sat in silence for a while, turning the venison with long twigs and at last eating some of it while the rest dried over red embers.

"Where will you go?" asked Shakochee.

"To Fort Brooke," replied Rod. "And you?"

"To the south, where my people now live."

"Will you be able to find them?"

"I will try."

Rod looked up quickly. "If you have trouble finding them, Shakochee, come to the fort. I'll tell them you're my friend, and there won't be any trouble."

Shakochee shook his head slowly. "I will fight with my people. You with yours."

Rod stared down at the cooking venison and did not answer. It was true. The white and the red were at war. No single friendship could matter when two nations fought with guns for the right to a piece of land. The injustice of it smote him as never before, but he did not speak of it, for there was nothing he could say.

"I hope I will never meet you in battle, Shakochee."

Shakochee looked at him squarely. "Should I see your face in the sight of my gun I will not fire."

"Nor I—if I should see you."

They did not talk any more. Soon after, they lay on the ground to sleep, and in the morning they went their separate ways, Rod to Tampa and Shakochee southeast. At their parting, they said only "Good-bye."

Chapter XVI

Tampa

"Thus ended the winter campaign of 1836. The regulars were ordered to summer quarters and the volunteers discharged and sent home."

—JOHN LEE WILLIAMS
in *Territory of Florida*

Rod and his brother, Hughie, were shucking oysters in the shadow of the house on Tampa Bay. It was the same house in which the Wheelers had found refuge when war broke, only now, in June, the stockade across the rear of the property was complete, with loopholes for guns and a lookout post at one corner. So far, the place had not been used as a fort, but with General Scott's armies disbanded for the summer and the Indians active as ever, Rod's father said trouble might come any day.

Both boys glanced up as a boat ground against the sand at the water's edge.

"Pa's back from shrimping," observed Rod, "we'd best finish quick."

"Who's with him?" asked Hughie, staring at the four men in the boat.

Rod stared, too. His father and his Uncle Ace he recognized instantly. But he wasn't sure about the other two. Could one of them be John Fox? As the man came closer, Rod saw that it was John. And the other—the tall, stringy fellow with a haggard face—suddenly looked like Hart Whitley, lean, tired.

Rod shouted a welcoming "Hello," wiped his fishy hands on his pants and ran to meet the visitors. His grin-lighted face brought an answering smile from Hart.

The boy's excitement showed in the vigorous pumping he gave the scout's arm. "You made it!" he kept crying, over and over. "Tell us everything that happened!"

"Just a minute, Rod," said his father reprovingly. "Hart's going to stay to supper and you'll have plenty of time to talk to him. Right now he wants to speak to Mother and Aunt Cele. And you've some more oysters to shuck, if I'm not mistaken."

Rod gulped down his curiosity and hurried back to his job. When he and Hughie had finished, they washed up and joined the four men, who had seated themselves for a smoke on benches outside the cabin door.

There was no more bench room, so the boys sat on the ground, Rod eying Hart and wondering when his uncle would stop talking about the weather. At the first pause in the conversation, he said eagerly: "Tell us now, Hart! What happened on the Withlacoochee?"

"Let's hear what happened to *you*," retorted Hart. "I thought you were a goner. How'd you get home in such fine shape?"

Rod flushed, for he did not like to talk about himself. But he started, back at the canoe incident, and hastily sketched the story of his trip south. When he had finished, Hart said shortly, "The slave catchers have caused a good bit of our trouble with the Indians. I hate to say it of any man, but Sam Ruther is better dead than alive."

The others agreed quietly, and Hughie broke into the silence. "Now tell us how you got to the Suwannee, Hart. What happened to that fellow with the funny name—Kettles or suchlike."

"Potts—Tom Potts," corrected Hart gently. "A funny name—and to some folks a funny man—but a finer one never entered the Territory of Florida. He's still up on the Suwannee, sick of fever."

"Not bad, is he?" asked Rod anxiously, for the fever had killed many men, and he wanted Tom Potts to live.

"He's well over the worst," Hart assured him.

"Good," said Rod, relieved. "Now let's hear what the two of you did with the overturned canoe. Did you get it right side up and back into the water?"

"That we did," said Hart, "even though all our corn was lost; our guns in the bottom of the river, and our powder wet as mud. We didn't have any paddles, either, but we were so glad to have the boat we'd have stroked her with our bare hands."

"Did you?" put in Hughie, fascinated with the idea.

"Of course," replied John Fox, his eyes gleaming with humor. "Hart can do anything."

The scout smiled. "After we'd floated down river a ways, we stopped and cut some paddles. They were just stubby sticks flattened out a little, but they took us to the mouth of the Withlacoochee."

"See any more Indians?" asked Rod quickly.

"Not until we got to the Suwannee. Then we were shot at again, but we got through without a scratch to Major Read's post. He took us back up the Withlacoochie and moved every man out of the blockhouse—didn't lose a single soldier."

"That's good—good," observed Rod's father. "But look, Hart, how'd those fellows get stuck up there in the first place? Do you reckon they got their orders wrong—or what happened?"

Hart was slow to answer. He puffed his pipe to a bright glow and let it die. At last he said: "As nearly as I can make out, that was pure fate. Major McLemore, who led the detachment, left it to go back to the Suwannee. He promised to bring relief. On the way he took a fever and died. Everybody else was busy with his own affairs, and the garrison was forgotten."

"Forgotten!" exclaimed John Fox. "Neglected through plain carelessness, you mean." He chewed indignantly at his pipe. "General Scott knew the detachment was going up the river. He knew a depot was planned. He should have sent some relief —or at least orders to come back."

"I believe there was misunderstanding as to the orders," mused Hart. "The death of McLemore . . ."

"It will all come out when General Scott's campaign is investigated by Congress," said John Fox tartly, "and that it will be."

"There were many difficulties," suggested Hart.

"He should have expected those. And now this insane business of postponing the war during the summer—it's fantastic. It gives the Indians time to grow new crops of corn and peas, to gather more ammunition and run more bullets. And don't think Osceola won't be encouraged, too, after this breathing spell."

Hart was stubborn in his contention that Scott had tried hard. "But just when he was getting started, the militias from other states were ready to go home," he reminded them. "And it wasn't his fault that he didn't know Florida." When no one spoke, he added, "But his mistakes will help our next general."

Mr. Wheeler groaned. "More fighting—yes, I suppose there will be. Nothing really has been changed by this spring campaign."

"Not a thing," agreed John Fox shortly, "except that a lot of money was spent and a lot of men died."

Hughie looked up at Hart. "You said last fall that we might never beat the Indians. Do you still think that, Hart?"

Hart did not smile as he answered. His lean face was somber. "I still think it, Hughie."

#369